"I'm all right."

But Emily longed to throw off responsibilities for the day and enjoy a nice afternoon with Darin and the kids.

"Hang on a minute, Emily. I'm going to ask Pastor Fredericks to drive the boys home."

"No!" the kids whined in unison.

"No, Darin. I need to get to work. Really." But she was about as convincing as a two-year-old turning down candy. Darin laughed at her and crossed his arms at her lack of conviction.

She sat there, staring at the steering wheel, and soon Darin returned without his inner city boys' club.

He opened her door. "Get into the passenger seat. I'm driving."

Emily didn't argue.

KRISTIN BILLERBECK lives in California's beautiful Gold Country with her husband and four small children. Besides writing, Kristin loves reading, outings with her family, and eating out! Visit her on the web at: www.kristinbillerbeck.com Or email her at: KrisBeck@aol.com

Books by Kristin Billerbeck

HEARTSONG PRESENTS
HP247—Strong as the Redwood
HP294—To Truly See
HP329—Meet My Sister, Tess
HP378—The Landlord Takes a Bride
HP448—The Prodigal Welcome
HP454—Grace In Action

An Unbreakable Hope

Kristin Billerbeck

Heartsong Presents

To Aunt Mary
You are such an inspiration to everyone around you.
I love you more than I can say and appreciate all the
love you have shared with me and my children.
Now, fight for all it's worth! God is with you.

A note from the Author:
I love to hear from my readers! You may correspond with me
by writing:

> **Kristin Billerbeck**
> **Author Relations**
> **PO Box 719**
> **Uhrichsville, OH 44683**

ISBN 1-58660-925-4

AN UNBREAKABLE HOPE

Our mission is to publish and distribute inspirational products offering exceptional value and biblical encouragement to the masses.

All scripture quotations, unless otherwise indicated, are taken from the HOLY BIBLE, NEW INTERNATIONAL VERSION®. NIV®. Copyright © 1973, 1978, 1984 by International Bible Society. Used by permission of Zondervan Publishing House. All rights reserved.

All of the characters and events in this book are fictitious. Any resemblance to actual persons, living or dead, or to actual events is purely coincidental.

one

"May I present to you for the first time, Mr. and Mrs. Mike Kingston." The preacher's voice boomed and Emily Jensen winced. Kingston. She had practiced the name Emily Kingston in her journal many times, but that name now belonged to Grace. To Grace, Mike, and Josh Kingston. They were a family now.

Emily's heart clenched. Not for the loss of Mike, for that hurt had been shallow and over with months ago, but for the loss of her dreams. Again. It felt as though every time she reached for marriage and a family, the balloon of hope got more distant, the string floated farther away. Disappointment shimmied through her frame. The piteous glances of the other wedding guests bored through her. *One more wedding where Emily wasn't the bride. What is wrong with that poor girl?* Their eyes told her what they were thinking, and she felt her body slink down further into the pew.

"I'm so sorry, Dear." Mrs. Purcell rubbed Emily's shoulder as if they faced an open casket rather than a stunning bride and groom.

"What's to be sorry about, Mrs. Purcell? Aren't Grace and Mike the happiest couple you've seen in ages? And look at little Josh. A stonecutter couldn't wipe the smile from his face."

"I know, but, Dear, it could have been you."

Tears threatened to spill once again, but Emily swallowed

them whole. It wasn't about Mike. Anyone could see from the way he watched Grace that there was no substitute for that kind of love. Emily coveted it, and yet it slipped through her hands like mercury again and again. She didn't want to be a man's second best, but would she ever be someone's first? The hope of such dreams was quickly fading with each birthday and failed relationship. It wasn't that she'd ever loved a man so thoroughly that her heart was broken in two; it was that no one had ever loved her either. Not in the way that causes long-term emotion. She discreetly wiped her eyes.

Emily held the withered hands that reached out to her. "Mrs. Purcell, I'm very busy with teaching. My class and my Sunday school kids need me. God called some to remain single, and I guess I'm one of them. Like Paul, I will be content in all situations." Her tone was strong—so much so she could almost believe herself. The truth was she'd never imagined being a parent to twenty schoolchildren without having one of her own. A husband to come home to and a child who looked up with wide eyes and called her Mommy, not Miss Jensen. She was angry at herself for not being content with the life God had blessed her with.

"That's the spirit, my dear. Those children love you, and you're a wonderful teacher." After a supplicating pat, Mrs. Purcell went to darken someone else's door with her words of doom. Emily breathed relief. The first test had been passed and no tears shed. So maybe a few had pooled, but not one had fallen. Indeed, now she felt a bit stronger.

She made her way toward the back of the church where Mike and Grace stood with Josh, a testimony to the glow a real family presented. Grace's dress flowed elegantly to the floor, a spray of white silk. Blonde tendrils hung in ringlets from a high-swept updo, and Grace's long, lean neck moved like that of a princess. That kind of beauty was rare, for Grace's beauty went beyond the exterior.

Emily moved toward them. "Grace, you are the most beautiful bride I've ever seen. Mike, you are one very lucky man."

Mike, in full fireman's dress uniform, kissed her cheek. "Thank you, Emily. I'm so glad you came today. It wouldn't have been the same without you here."

Josh, Grace's son, looked up and nodded. "You're still my favorite teacher even though I'm in second grade."

Emily winked. "Let's keep that our little secret, okay? I'll see you at the reception. You were a very good ring bearer. The best I've seen, in fact."

Emily hiked her shoulders back and walked resolutely toward the church event hall.

Test two completed. No tears shed.

The short walk across the open courtyard to the reception filled Emily with more confidence. Churchgoers and Mike's fellow firemen milled about, waiting for the reception line and photographs to be completed. Twinkling lights and floral sprays gave the old church hall a fresh feel, a romantic buzz. Emily could barely believe the old church hall was capable of such beauty. As she made her way toward the punch table, a handsome stranger handed her a glass.

"Thirsty?" he asked.

She felt her stomach tumble at the question. For a moment, she heard only silence as she stared into his eyes—eyes that accepted her into a world deemed off-limits. What she was feeling was akin to waking up in Wonderland. She felt like she had known this stranger her entire life, yet her mother would never let this kind of man near her.

Emily nodded and took the cup of red liquid.

"Do I know you?" she asked, feeling inept the moment the words escaped.

"You do now. Darin Black." The stranger's eyes were remarkable. Although they were a nondescript gray-green, the intensity that flared within them made them absolutely mesmerizing. His eyes extended some unmistakable compassion within him. She felt a sudden peace, completely forgetting she was at the wedding of an ex-boyfriend.

Darin's head was shaved bald, but from his eyebrows and stubble upon his head, Emily could see a natural light red shade. She felt her own eyes widen at the unexpected sight of an earring. Never in all her days had she known a man to wear an earring. She studied it a bit too long, and he commented.

"The earring?"

She choked back her punch. "Was I that obvious?" Emily looked around at all the well-dressed firemen and regular churchgoers then back to the stranger. His suit was just a gray tweed sports coat over navy slacks, but the earring threw the whole look off for Emily. She pondered the statement the jewelry made before answering. Perhaps it should have mattered that he wore the earring, but it didn't. It only made her more curious about whom he was. Why he was at Mike's wedding, and whether he knew her sordid tale. Realizing her long silence, she blurted, "I've never met a man with an earring before." She was tempted to ask if he was a gang member but quickly thought better of the idea. Emily Post would not have approved.

"Never met a man with an earring? What a sheltered life you've led." His smile was captivating. So much so she almost forgot about the jewelry. But then her eyes were drawn back to the simple silver stud. There was something pirate-like about it. Something attractive that she didn't want to admit to liking. It was too strange. Her mother certainly wouldn't approve. Maybe that explained Emily's fascination, but there was something in his eyes. It wasn't a feeling she recognized, but something familiar to her all the same.

She cleared her throat; it was probably best to avoid the subject of the earring. "How do you know the bride and groom?"

"Mike pulled me out of a gutter one night."

"I beg your pardon?"

"I had a sports car in my wilder days. Let me stress the word had. I crashed it against a tree. Mike was the attending fireman who pulled me out of the mangled steel. Been my good friend ever since."

Emily was subconsciously retreating from the shadow this man cast under the twinkling aura of tea lights. Fear wasn't what she felt; it was an intense curiosity, and that's what scared her. She'd never met anyone like him, much less in the church hall. Dangerous. He felt dangerous, so why did she want to know more? And why did she feel a security standing beside him?

"Mike led me to the Lord in the hospital, after I saw my life flash before my eyes and God called me from my stupidity." The corner of his mouth lifted, and he was obviously waiting for some semblance of a response.

"The Lord can do mighty things." Emily closed her eyes

at her easy statement to his incredible testimony. What a hack she was.

"Amen."

"I grew up in the church." She supposed that probably needed no explanation. The floral dress with the lace collar and sheer lip gloss probably gave her away. She looked like she grew up in the church, and suddenly she felt herself fingering her collar wishing she'd bought something more stylish for the wedding. Would it have killed her to buy a new outfit? Certainly not anything leather, but a trendy outfit from a store—maybe even nice slacks.

"What a blessing for you to grow up in the church. You should thank God for that every day." His enthusiasm wasn't forced, and he was shaking his head at the thought. "I'm so excited that my kids will be able to start better than I did. I can hardly wait to do family devotionals and teach them everything I can about the Lord. Not just the simple stories, mind you, like the flood or Jonah, but all of it. I want them to crave the Word."

She blinked rapidly, hoping he hadn't noticed how attractive she found him. He had kids. Children were just a ticket to Emily's heart; unfortunately for her, wives usually went with them.

"How many kids do you have?" She held her breath at his answer.

"Me?" He laughed. "I don't have any kids. I'm not married."

A spring rain of relief washed over Emily, but she couldn't have said why. This man reminded her of someone who was brave enough to preach on the street. To walk into a homeless shelter and feel perfectly comfortable. God had a man for her. A man carefully groomed in the church. The man her father prayed for every day during her childhood. And certainly that man didn't wear an earring or crash sports cars. Emily felt her breath leave her. Would that man make her heart pound like this one did?

"Well, I'm sure your family will be very fortunate when God brings children to you."

"Thank you."

Emily scanned the room for someone she knew, looking for an escape route. The best way to avoid temptation was to stay away from it. Even Mrs. Purcell would be a welcome reprieve. This man, handsome in a movie star way, unnerved her. He was too good-looking for his own good. Too intense for hers. His bold pronouncements of faith were something akin to a weekend revival in the South. Nothing like her reserved, quiet faith that lived its life out in consistency.

"It was very nice to meet you. Maybe I'll see you around church sometime."

"We haven't actually met," his outstretched hand extended toward her. "I've told you my name is Darin Black, but I haven't heard yours."

"Emily Jensen."

"The Emily Jensen?"

She swallowed hard. "What do you mean by that?" As if she didn't know.

"You're the one Mike used to see. Before he met Grace. You helped bring Grace around, right?"

Where was a plastic fern when she needed one? Emily wished she could crawl under the table and disappear. She'd passed the first two tests, but this one proved impossible.

Tears began to sting her eyes. She blinked them away as fast as she could.

"You know, I'm thinking maybe I've outstayed my welcome here. I need to get my lesson plans ready for Monday, and Mike and Grace have plenty of guests to celebrate with them." Emily moved quickly for the door, but she could feel Darin Black behind her, even hear his steps. She quickened her pace but felt her hand grasped. She whirled around, tears now apparent upon her cheeks. "Please, Mr. Black. I'm sure you'll understand if I just want to go home. I'm very pleased for Grace and Mike, but the church knows our story and you can imagine this is uncomfortable for me. Being the 'other woman' at a church wedding is hardly a good feeling."

His eyes met hers, and she lost all sight of the earring. There was only this gorgeous man peering down at her with compassion and concern. "Emily, you were never the other woman. I didn't mean it that way. Only that Mike raves about you because you helped Grace to find the Lord when he hadn't treated you as well. I'm an idiot. Forgive me."

She just shook her head. Words wouldn't come. *Mike remembers me for my words to Grace?* She wanted to shout, but she couldn't get past the lump in her throat for fear she'd start blubbering.

"Would you like to have dinner with me tonight? I'm not trying to hit on you, I just don't want to leave you with this bad impression, and I know this is a difficult night. This is going to sound very strange, but I feel like I know you. I want to know you better."

No, she said via gesture. "Home."

"Please, let's go get some dinner together. We can have

church potluck anytime. Mrs. Purcell's chicken will still be rubbery," he laughed. "Here, wait. . .Pastor," and he pulled unwitting Pastor Fredericks toward them. "Tell Emily I'm a good guy. That I'm safe to be with and that I won't stick her with the bill."

Pastor Fredericks smiled at them both, and Emily swallowed the guilt she felt. *No, I'm not swallowing up another man with my black widow ways, Pastor Fredericks. I promise.*

"You're in good hands, Emily. Darin is an upstanding gentleman with a big heart for the Lord," he said. "Go enjoy your Friday evening. The excitement is over here. Mike and Grace are leaving tonight for Carmel, so they'll have to get a move-on." He checked his watch. "They only have the weekend and then they're back to work and school for Josh. You two have a lot in common."

Emily looked up at the shaved head, the steely gray-green eyes, and of course the earring. What she could have in common with such a man remained a mystery to her. But she trusted her pastor, and Darin did offer her an escape from the reception, where the deaconesses of the church had staged a pity party for her. They were coming toward her in a gaggle.

Pastor continued. "Emily, why don't you take him to that soup house you're always frequenting. Every time I go in there you're sitting there with a book. They're open late and Darin can probably afford that." He winked at Darin.

She almost kissed him. So he could have left off the part about eating there alone with her book, but other than that, she wasn't ready for this night to end. She wasn't ready to ignore this connection she felt with a complete stranger. She'd feel safe at the soup house. The owners knew her and loved her. They started her order before she sat down. The Vietnamese soup house would be a perfect place to have a friendly dinner with this different kind of man. Her stomach was flipping, and she hoped she could find the control to eat.

"That's a wonderful idea, Pastor. It's up the street from here on Castro. Do you know the place?" she asked Darin.

"Sure," he nodded. "I'll meet you there so you don't have to drive with a stranger. Is that all right with you?"

His thoughtfulness nettled her, and she nodded in agreement. But her comfort gave way to trepidation in her car. What on earth was she doing? Meeting a strange man for dinner with Pastor's approval. It was so out of character for her, and yet so exciting. What would her mother say? For the moment, she didn't care. The fluttering she felt in her stomach was new.

৯

In the brightly lit restaurant, Darin studied Emily Jensen, her chocolate-brown eyes rimmed in red. Her exterior was so simple in her plain dress, but Darin could see the depth within her soul. She may wear an easy churchgoing façade, but Darin believed he saw an explosive spark within, that glimmer of light that wanted to come out and dance before the Lord, but didn't know how—an untapped missionary's heart. He knew what she probably thought of him, but that didn't stop him from wanting to know her. She felt the immediate communion between them too, or she wouldn't have been so tongue-tied.

"That was a nice wedding, don't you think?" Darin asked.

Emily nodded.

"So I hear you're a teacher."

Emily nodded again. "Yes, I taught Grace's son Josh last year."

"Do you like teaching?" *Come on, Emily, help me out here.* Darin tapped his foot, hoping to end this sudden uneasiness between them. No longer were they in the safety of their congregation. Now they were officially on a date, and Emily looked everywhere about the restaurant but at him.

"I love teaching the children. I teach on Sundays as well. I have the second- and third- graders."

Emily still wouldn't look at him when she spoke, and his heart hurt at the reminder that he wasn't the type such an innocent would marry. She probably imagined he dated Camaro-driving, stiletto-heeled women. He winced at the thought of his former life. Emily's beauty went beyond her lovely dark hair and espresso eyes, and into her innocent expression of love for the Lord. Darin wanted the chance to prove his past life was over, and he wanted to be worthy of such a pure woman. Would someone like Emily Jensen ever look his way?

He cleared his throat. "Since you're working in Sunday school maybe I'll see you. I just started work with the junior high ministry. I've been bringing some kids from the inner city. I work with them on Wednesdays, playing pickup basketball and then having a Bible study in a garage."

"I've never been to the inner city. What's it like?"

"I thought you grew up here."

"I did." Emily blinked, clearly not understanding his point.

"You grew up within a couple miles of East Palo Alto, and you've never been there?"

"My mother always warned me not to go there." Emily shrugged.

He leaned in, and she sat straight up in her chair. "Didn't that make you want to go there? To find out what was so bad about it? People are the same, only the circumstances are different."

She shook her head. "Of course that didn't make me want to go. It wasn't a good part of town. It still isn't a good part of town. What more do I need to know?"

"Emily, EPA is a ripe mission field. There are people there who live in absolute squalor, yet know the Lord is with them always. Their joy in the Lord is like nothing you've ever seen here in Los Altos. It's practiced with abandon. These people know peace in all circumstances. Don't you think that's admirable?"

"Not if it means going where it's dangerous. I'm not really very adventurous. I like knowing my surroundings well."

Darin's heart sank at the shaky fear in Emily's voice. Didn't she know God would protect her? He probably should have kept his thoughts to himself, but he blurted, "Fear is the work of the evil one. God says not to be anxious for anything. That means when there are bullets flying in your neighborhood, you can rest in Him."

"There's a line between trusting the Lord and doing stupid things like going into a dangerous place and expecting Him to rescue me."

Her words pierced him. Their soup arrived, but Darin wasn't hungry. The vigor and life he thought he'd seen in Emily had quickly disappeared behind her love for safety. Darin's life was bold. From bungee jumping to street preaching, he lived dangerously. Where once it had been for the adrenaline rush, now it was for the sake of the gospel. After all, he'd almost been killed—anything after the crash was a gift from above. Darin prayed over the Vietnamese noodle soup, and they ate their meal in silence. Maybe this had been a mistake. It certainly wasn't an ideal first date. Darin peered at the golden liquid inside his bowl. *I'll never be a Christian in the proper churchsense of the word.*

two

Emily arrived early as usual on Sunday and straightened the Sunday school lessons and cut out all the necessary shapes for the craft. She lined everything up into neat rows so the students could easily access their take-home study. She loved it when parents continued the study at home during the week. It brought her immense joy to know her work was helping young Christians become grounded.

"There," she said aloud at the sight of her perfectly organized table.

"Hi." Darin Black leaned against the doorjamb, his broad shoulders filling the entrance to the classroom. Emily swallowed over her nervousness. She noticed as she lined up the papers again that her hands trembled. The pirate had returned, and she was unprepared for her reaction. She giggled nervously, like one of her first-graders.

"Hi," she said quietly. "Are you working with the junior-highers today?"

"I am, but first I have some of their little brothers I brought with me from town. They'll be in your class. This is Nicholas." Darin brought forward a little boy who looked like an overgrown puppy who hadn't developed into his paws yet. "He's only in the second grade. He's just the size of your average high schooler." Darin mussed the boy's hair.

Nicholas had a wary look to his eyes, and they thinned at

the sight of her, announcing his immediate defiance. Emily knew the look well from her years of teaching and looked forward to an eventful hour. She instantly felt thankful she taught in a nice part of town and didn't have to deal with this defiance on a regular basis. A few more of these kids, and her joy for teaching might dwindle quickly.

"And this," Darin added, "is Jason."

"The worm who cried when he left his Mama," Nicholas said tauntingly.

"Hey!" Darin lifted the corner of Nicholas's shirt. "You mess with him, you mess with me. Got it?"

Emily flinched at the harsh words. Echoes of her childhood chilled her, but when she looked at Darin he had a smile plastered on his face. He seemed almost serene and the boys both laughed.

She tried to put the boys at ease immediately, knowing her organized classroom and the well-coifed children probably made them feel uncomfortable. They each wore a cartoon T-shirt that most kids wouldn't be allowed to own in the church. The chasm between the children saddened her. No wonder so many visitors stopped coming. She prayed, hoping she could find the connection to keep the boys interested.

"Nicholas and Jason, it's nice to have you in my class. Would you like to color until we get started?" She handed them each a coloring sheet.

"Whatever." Nicholas rolled his eyes and pushed past her to a desk, where he flopped into the seat. He cursed as he hit his knee on the top of the metal. Darin apologized with his eyes. "I'm not three. I don't color."

"I also have building toys," Emily offered. She liked to

have cool things for the boys to do with their hands while they listened. She found it was far more effective than telling them to sit down countless times. So Legos were a regular feature in her classroom.

Jason said nothing but also ignored the coloring sheet. He crossed his arms over his chest. His hair hung over his eyes, hiding his true expression. Emily felt hopeless looking at him. The boy seemed to have no joy left in him. And although he wasn't more than eight, Legos were beyond childish to him. She pitied how fast these children had to grow up in the ghetto. Childhood never existed for them, judging by the hardness of their expressions or the coldness in their eyes.

She drew in a deep breath, and Darin said, "Don't take any of Nicholas's garbage. He needs this." With a wink implying collusion, he turned and walked toward the middle school class. A bevy of kids, including several giggling girls, followed him like the Pied Piper. Emily laughed at the sight, secretly wishing she could follow as well.

She turned back to her class. In all the commotion of her new students, she hadn't noticed that everyone had been signed in and now sat around the room, staring at the two new children like new animals at the zoo.

"Well," Emily said. "For those of you who don't know me, I'm Miss Jensen, and today we're going to learn about Cain and Abel—two brothers who had two different hearts toward God."

Nicholas raised a hand.

"Yes, Nicholas."

"I have to go to the bathroom."

"My teacher's aide isn't here yet, so you'll have to wait a bit." She didn't trust the boy to come back, so she needed to make sure he was chaperoned.

Again the boy cursed and reiterated his need to visit the bathroom in a coarse way. Although he was only eight or so, he frightened Emily with his harshness, and he probably sensed it. She'd never met a boy so young who acted in such a raw way, and visions of violent news footage played in her head. She shook her wild imagination.

"Nicholas, I'm telling you, we don't talk like that at church. Whether you believe it or not, there is a God listening, and He is not pleased. You can try to make me mad, but I wouldn't test God."

"I'm shaking." By now, all the children were mesmerized. They'd probably never witnessed such insolence, and in all Emily's years of teaching, she was certain she hadn't.

Nicholas jumped up on the desk and started dancing. "Tell God to come get me then!"

Almost as soon as he lifted a foot, he slipped from the desk and the back of his head hit another. Emily rushed across the room to where Nicholas lay crying. She was thankful for the jagged sounds, knowing that Nicholas was not knocked unconscious. He'd pulled into a fetal position and was screaming like an angry toddler, kicking the surrounding desks.

"Nicholas, show me where it hurts." Emily cradled his head and felt the knot on the back of his skull. Where was her teaching help? She scanned the room of wide-eyed children and selected the most mature of her kids. "Rachel, would you go find Mrs. Kless and tell her I need help. Quickly."

Rachel nodded and ran from the room with obvious relief.

Emily soothed Nicholas with soft words and asked the rest of the children to pray for the boy's head. He wasn't badly hurt. His ego was far more bruised than his head, but it was the way he cried. The childishness within him scared Emily. She'd heard this kind of explosive crying before, when a broken soul let the pain ooze freely. Suddenly, she saw Nicholas in a whole new light—as a broken heart rather than a defiant child.

She had to focus. She had to concentrate on the task at hand. She sat on the floor and pulled Nicholas onto her lap, which, surprisingly, he didn't fight. His body was rigid with distress. The class looked at her expectantly. She cleared her throat and began the lesson. She told the story of Cain and Abel while holding Nicholas. The children watched with wide, attentive eyes, fearful that Nicholas might rise or scream again.

Mrs. Kless came and took the children to another class for craft. For some reason Emily wasn't ready to relinquish Nicholas or Jason. The lost boys, as she now thought of them.

Nicholas's harsh look died, and she felt him relax in her arms, molding into her form. She looked up to see Darin's worried frown.

"Nicholas. You all right, Buddy?"

The boy ran to Darin and allowed the big man to embrace him like a baby. Jason watched the whole situation without saying a word.

Emily raked her hand through her hair. "I'm sorry, Darin." Her lips quivered, and she fought a wave of emotion. She'd done the right thing and remained calm, but she didn't feel that way. Everything within her didn't want to let go of the boys, to send them back to the adult world they lived in.

"I—" Her voice broke.

"Emily, what's the matter? It's just a little fall. Kids take falls all the time."

She bristled. "Yes, you're right." After Nicholas quieted down, Emily pulled Darin away. "I just wish there was something more I could do."

"When kids climb, they sometimes fall."

Mrs. Kless came in and brought a first-aid kit and an accident report for the church office. Emily calmly filled out the paperwork, but she didn't feel soothed in her heart. She regretted sending Nicholas back home to whatever pain he clutched. His cries over a fall would haunt her like the cries of her next-door neighbor as a child. She excused herself.

Free of teaching second hour, she ran across the parking lot and found her car. Fumbling with her keys, she unlocked the door and clambered into the driver's seat. Images of the handsome Darin Black—and her inability to teach a simple Sunday school class in front of him—filled her mind. She closed her eyes and imagined herself touching the soft red stubble on his shaved head. Maybe her subconscious believed his dangerous side was enough to rescue her from her loneliness. She'd thought the same of Mike, but he'd seen through her gentle façade. He'd seen the real Emily for who she really was, and he'd run away like a frightened fawn. No knight in shining armor was coming to rescue her. She needed to get over that dream and continue loving the kids God had given her to help: her students.

She didn't know how long she sat in the car, but when she looked around the parking lot was nearly empty. Darin rapped on her window, and she started at the sight of him with four young boys. Nicholas was one of them.

"We just wanted you to know that Nicholas was fine. He gave us a good scare, but he's a tough cookie. Aren't you, Bud?"

"Better believe it," Nicholas said with all the bravado of a high school quarterback.

"We're going to get some lunch before we head back to EPA. You want to join us?" Darin lifted his light red eyebrows, and the motion captivated Emily. So much so she forgot to answer.

"Emily?" he asked.

"Oh, I'm sorry. No, I've got to get my classroom ready for tomorrow."

"Working on a Sunday?" There was a hint of disappointment in his voice.

"I'm afraid a teacher's work is never done. I had to work the school fair yesterday, so I didn't get all my lesson plans finished."

"Em, this wasn't your fault, you know. Nicholas told me what happened and said he was sorry."

She just shook her head. "I know, but I was in charge and I feel badly that I let you down."

"Emily?"

She met his eyes and marveled again at their color—a slate gray-green that calmed the senses. It was the kind of color a hospital might use on the walls to lower blood pressure. It certainly lowered hers.

"Let me drive you home. Work can wait."

She still stared into his eyes, hoping for a little of the peace they seemed to emanate. How did someone who knew the Lord for such a short time possess such inner peace?

"I'm all right." But Emily longed to throw off all of her

responsibilities for the day and enjoy a nice afternoon with Darin and the kids.

"Hang on a minute, Emily. I'm going to ask Pastor Fredericks to drive the boys home."

"No!" the kids whined in unison.

"No, Darin. I need to get to work. Really." But she was about as convincing as a two-year-old turning down candy. Darin laughed at her and crossed his arms at her lack of conviction.

She sat there, staring at the steering wheel, and soon Darin returned without his inner city boys' club.

He opened her door. "Get into the passenger seat. I'm driving."

Emily didn't argue.

Darin gazed at her. "Emily, what's wrong? You seem to be making an awfully big deal of a kid falling and having to work on a Sunday. Are you trying to avoid me?"

"No." *Quite the contrary.* "I was just reminded today of something that happened a long time ago. Something I thought I'd sorted out with God. I didn't know how to handle a child like Nicholas. It never occurred to me as a child to defy the rules. Maybe I'd be more exciting if I had."

"Is it so surprising that you couldn't handle Nicholas?"

"I'm a teacher."

"In the middle of Mansion Row, Emily. You're a teacher for spoiled rich kids. In contrast, these kids saw a slasher flick last night, and they were pretending to knife each other when I picked them up this morning. That something you're used to?" He fought off laughter.

Emily shuddered. "How can you protect them when you take them out?"

"I do my best. I keep a close eye on them, but ultimately the Lord has to care for them the rest of the week. Their mothers all work two jobs or more. Most of the kids don't know who their fathers are. I can only be a piece in God's puzzle for them. I can't be everything." He paused for a moment, looking deeply into her eyes. "And neither can you."

But she wondered about that. Wasn't being there for the kids exactly what she was called to do?

Darin started her car. He turned out of the parking lot and headed away from her home.

"Where are we going?"

"You need to get some food into you. You're happier when you're full, at least I am. There's a nice little breakfast place downtown."

As the car approached the city, Emily thought the restaurant was better described as a greasy spoon. Clearly, being a Christian wasn't the only definition they disagreed upon.

"This place has the best eggs benedict you'll ever eat," Darin said as the hostess motioned toward a vinyl-covered booth.

Somehow I doubt that, Emily thought.

"The usual?" the waitress asked.

"Two please. Emily, what do you want to drink?"

"Just iced water." Thinking better of her choice, she said, "Make that a Diet Pepsi." In Mexico, they always warned you not to drink the water. Somehow Emily thought that might be good advice for this restaurant.

The waitress grabbed the menus and left. Emily was grateful Darin had taken over for the moment. She found herself staring at him again. He was so beautiful. Not a word you'd use to describe a man, but it fit Darin to a T. Movie-star gorgeous with a dash of danger.

"What are your parents like?" she asked, wondering what terrible stories he could tell of living with ungodly parents.

"They're good people. They don't know the Lord, but they gave me every opportunity to make something of myself. Albeit, without much guidance. I was pretty much free to do as I liked. I had a basketball scholarship to college, but I quickly squandered it when I discovered the college life could be so much fun."

Emily crossed her arms, sinking into the booth. "College was fun?"

"No," Darin laughed. "College wasn't fun, but all the extracurricular activities were. So much so I flunked out. That's why I'm doing landscape work now. I was in a five-year program for architecture. I got enough engineering to design a great sprinkler and lawn system. But not much else, other than how to down a six-pack in six minutes."

Emily mentally calculated the strikes against Darin Black based on her mother's list of qualities to look for in a man. He was a college dropout, former street racer, and former drinker. There was the issue of the earring and the fact that he was comfortable in the inner city, not to mention this dive restaurant.

Staring at this gentle man across from her, it was hard to believe all she knew about him was true. She rubbed the back of her neck, wondering what she might say to keep normal conversation flowing. She didn't feel like conversing. She just wanted to go to the school and try harder to be the teacher she should be. And she wanted to ignore her growing feelings for a man who would not meet the approval of her parents.

"You're quiet, Emily." Darin lifted her chin slightly with his thumb. It was the first time he'd touched her, and her body betrayed her. She felt his touch to her toes. "It's okay if you don't feel like talking. Just sit back and enjoy breakfast. I'm content to look at the beautiful view." He winked at her. "I'm really sorry if the boys were too much for you."

Emily shook her head. "No, the boys weren't too much. They just reminded me of something Fireman Mike once told me." She paused for a moment. "He said I couldn't rescue the world. But I wonder if I could rescue anyone?"

Darin kept those green eyes upon her, and she felt the need to keep talking.

"I can try harder, but those words haunt me. If I'm not good at teaching, what's my purpose?"

He smiled. "I don't believe it for a second. What could haunt the zealous Miss Emily Jensen?"

She forced her eyes away to the baseball game that blared from a mounted TV set. A hit cracked on the television, and cheers from the restaurant patrons drowned out her answer. "What indeed."

three

Darin stared at Emily's apartment for a long time after dropping her off. They'd switched cars back at the church parking lot, but he had insisted on seeing her safely home. He wished he'd stayed in the classroom to help her with the boys. She loved children, that was obvious, and he certainly hadn't meant to overwhelm her with the boys. Her background must have been so free of troubles growing up with a strong Christian family. It wasn't like his, where he'd seen some terrible things on the street. Emily had been protected her whole life, and he just couldn't imagine what warranted her fears that she was an inadequate teacher. He scratched the back of his head and finally pulled away in his car.

His parents were expecting him for early supper, but he didn't feel up to it. Ever since he'd become a Christian, life with his parents had become strained. Darin wanted them in heaven with him, but his parents saw it as another crazy fad. Just like his sports cars and brief college stint. Darin sighed. It was up to God and beyond his own control, but that didn't mean he'd stop telling them about Jesus. The name of Jesus was harsher than the word God in his parents' home. The holiness of it evoked strong responses.

As he pulled into their driveway, his stomach lurched. In front of the house sat Angel's flashy red convertible. His old girlfriend. A woman who knew how to pull his strings. Any man's strings, in fact. He thought about running. Didn't God say to flee dangerous situations? But how would that prove to his parents that he was different now? His mother obviously thought Angel could rescue him from what she called his "religious phase."

He took a minute to bathe himself in prayer before he approached the front door. Before his hand touched the knob, the door swung open and Angel Mallory stood at the threshold. All five-feet-eight of her. He was surprised that her image didn't cause the usual response in him. What he felt now was more akin to disgust than lust.

She wore a too-tight T-shirt and form-fitting jeans that were cut low. Too low for decency's sake. Her smile was welcoming, inviting and purposeful. Darin gulped.

"Angel," he said as calmly as possible.

"That's all you have to say to me?" She put a hand to her hip then came toward him and wrapped him in a hug. He remained stiff and pulled away quickly.

"Nice to see you again." Darin walked right past her and kissed his mother on the cheek. "Hi, Mom. You didn't tell me you were having company."

"Honey, did you say hello to Angel properly?"

"I did." Darin flashed her an impromptu smile. "I hugged her." Actually, Angel had hugged him, but he wasn't splitting hairs now.

"Hey, Darin." His dad lifted a bottled beer toward him. "You want one? Giants are playing."

"How about a root beer instead?" A soda and baseball. That, he could handle. Not to mention that the game provided the necessary escape route.

He left Angel to help his mother without any semblance of guilt. She had invited Angel; she could entertain the woman. Darin had tried to speak with Angel about the changes in his life. He'd tried to get her to go to church, but she'd only laughed at him and called him weak, relying on religion to do his thinking for him. The sting still hurt. He was stronger now than he'd ever been.

Angel had paraded various men in front of him, to let him know she was still attractive. A man would have to be blind not to notice Angel's outer beauty, but Darin failed to see anything beautiful within her now. She was like a train wreck waiting to happen. He still prayed for her every day, asking for forgiveness if he'd done anything to initiate her fall. They'd only dated for two short months, but God started speaking to him in that time, and as God's light became more apparent, Angel's darkness became ever bleaker.

"The game's boring," his dad said.

"Baseball's always a little slow, Dad."

"You wouldn't think so if you didn't try all those extreme sports. Bungee jumping," his father said, shaking his head. "If man was meant to jump from a bridge, we would have been made with rubber feet. Or should I say heads."

Darin laughed. "Don't worry, Dad, my bungee jumping days are through. I'm moving to EPA now, and I don't want to set a bad example for the kids."

Ray Black clicked off the television set. "You are what?"

"I'm going to move with the ministry team there, Dad. I'm going to live in a house with some guys to work with the kids. I'll still be doing the landscaping during the day."

"Are you nuts? Those kids are someone else's problem, not

yours. Sometimes I think you were born with rocks for brains." He kept shaking his head, his disapproval more than obvious. "Where did we go wrong with you? What did we do to make you think you have to live like a martyr? So you didn't get through college, that ain't no crime. I've done just fine without college. Got me a nice house, big-screen TV, a camper for long weekends. Why don't you set a goal instead of trying to save the world?"

"Dad, this has nothing to do with education. As a matter of fact, one of my new roommates graduated from Stanford, and the other has his master's degree from Princeton. This is about me doing what God is asking me to do."

The comment only set his father off. "If God is talking to you now, I'd rather have you bungee jumping than listening to voices!"

"Dinner's ready!" his mother called.

Darin sat on the sofa for a moment and was surprised where his thoughts went. Not to the kids, not to his new home, but to Emily. He saw her face and longed for her comfort and understanding in this situation. Could Emily deal with a man like him? Accept him with all his mistakes and wrong turns? When she'd stayed on the straight and narrow path, and Darin had done everything but follow the right road?

Angel stood in the doorway, her belly peeking out between her jeans and short tee. He wanted to ask her if that was supposed to be attractive, but he snapped his mouth shut. It was better if she thought he hadn't noticed.

"Let's eat," his father said.

Everyone gathered around the table, and Darin silently

offered up a word of thanks and asked for help in getting through the uncomfortable meal. His father was now livid, his mother thought him incredibly rude to Angel, and Angel herself sat waiting for him to say something.

His mother took the opportunity to pass the green beans and elbow him in the process. "Talk to her."

"So your mom tells me you're still in that cult of Jesus freaks." Angel stifled a giggle.

Darin looked down at his plate, focusing on the mountain of mashed potatoes. He bit back a sarcastic comment and stuffed potatoes in his mouth instead. It wouldn't do him any good to attack. It would only reflect badly on him and his faith.

"Angel is trying out for the Raiderettes!" his mother announced brightly. Could she truly want a professional cheerleader for a daughter-in-law? The whole subject mystified him. What did his mother see in Angel that kept their friendship going long after Darin knew there was no point to a relationship? The only thing he and Angel had had in common was the club scene and their red sports cars. Now they had nothing in common. Nothing but this dinner table anyway.

It was hard to see Angel as a person without seeing her as a symbol of all he had left behind. It wasn't that he felt above her, it was that he feared falling backwards into the life that had him by the throat for so long. Angel was like a beautiful casket, inviting him for a visit without escape. He actually shivered thinking about it.

"The Raiderettes, huh? A lot of my boys from the neighborhood are big fans of the Raiders. You'll have to let me know how it goes. Maybe I could bring the boys to a game."

"Maybe next week you could go watch the tryouts, Darin."

His mother nodded her head briskly. "Angel is in the finals, so you won't have to watch all those amateurs."

"I'm kinda seeing someone, Mom. I don't think she'd appreciate me watching a bunch of professional cheerleaders." *Jesus wouldn't appreciate me watching a bunch of half-dressed aerobics instructors.* He looked at Angel. "No offense, of course. That's exciting news. I'm very proud of you."

The look on Angel's face was one of outrage. Darin wished he could take back his words, which she probably heard as judgmental and harsh. Her narrowed eyes made her motives painfully obvious. Angel didn't want him. She wanted him to want her. When his interest faltered, her desperation for his attention grew. Why else would she be sitting here over roast beef and mashed potatoes making small talk about professional cheerleading?

"Seeing someone?" Color drained from his mother's face. She lifted her plate from the table, throwing the silverware with a clang. She started to clear the dishes from the table, though no one was finished eating. "You never told me you were seeing someone."

"I just started seeing her, Mom. It's nothing serious yet. She's—" He started to say not like the other girls he'd dated but quickly refrained. "She's very special to me, and I just think it's something I want to follow through on."

"What does she do?" Angel smirked. "She's a model I bet." Her eyes mere slits, Darin felt like a trapped rat in a gutter. Nothing about his relationship with Emily could be considered truly "seeing her" except what Darin felt in his heart. To explain that would have made his parents question his sanity even more.

"She teaches first grade."

Angel cackled out loud and his mom joined her.

"You are dating a teacher? You, who never listened to a teacher in your life?"

"We're seeing each other, Mom. I don't know if we're at the dating stage yet." *But I want to be.*

His mother sat beside him and cupped his hand in hers. "I don't want you to be hurt. Does she know you're a college dropout? Is this one of those church girls? You know, church girls generally marry church boys."

Darin nodded.

"Oh, Honey." She looked at his dad. "Talk to him, Ray. Won't you?"

"He's never listened to me either, Mabel."

Angel stood. "I'd better go. I've got an aerobics class to teach." She shot Darin a lethal glance and exited quickly. His parents both sat back in their chairs, crossing their arms.

"Did you have to hurt her feelings like that?" his mother said.

"I wasn't trying to hurt her feelings, but I am seeing someone. You're the one who invited her here."

"Because I thought my son knew his manners. Honestly! Talking about another woman in Angel's presence. There will come a day when you regret that move. None of these church girls know who you really are, Darin Black. Angel loves the real Darin, just like we do."

Darin's thoughts drifted to Emily Jensen. Who was he kidding to think he was worthy of a woman like her? Angel's forced smile reminded him of all he'd been. And though Christ had washed away his sins, had He taken away the consequences that made him unworthy of Emily? He couldn't help but wonder.

❧

Emily cleaned her apartment until she thought the paint would erode under the pressure. The work made her forget what a fool she'd been earlier in the day to thumb her nose at a nice breakfast with Darin. It certainly beat all the meals she ate alone, yet in her own judgmental way she'd probably sent him a clear message. She ripped off the plastic glove and rubbed her forehead. She felt like she was back in high school. Darin Black was the popular kid, and she was still the gawky teen who didn't know what to say or how to dress. Being cool eluded her. Apparently, it was a lifetime legacy.

Why did she care if Darin thought she was crazy? He was a college dropout. He worked with his hands, she kept telling herself, trying to add disdain to the voice. But his heart. There was something so beckoning about a man who would minister in the ghetto, a man who would give up his own life to tell others about Jesus. Her Sunday school teaching felt pale in comparison. And then there was the small matter of what his appearance did to her heart.

She made herself an artichoke and plopped a big helping of mayonnaise beside it. Grabbing a bottled iced tea from the refrigerator, she settled down in front of the television. She killed a few channels before realizing she'd have to get something decent to watch. Placing a romantic video in the player, she settled back in when the phone rang.

"Hello," Emily answered.

"Emily, it's Darin."

Her stomach twisted and she put the plate on the coffee table, as if he could see her eating an artichoke. Somehow the vegetable didn't feel very feminine, and she was instantly embarrassed. All her mother's prodding came back to her. "Don't let a man see you eat." She laughed at the Scarlett O'Hara advice, but, sadly, some of it stuck, and the artichoke seemed like eating barbecue at Twelve Oaks.

"Hi, Darin." She wanted to ask how his afternoon went, what his parents had to say, what he had for dinner, but she clamped her mouth shut for fear she'd babble.

"Have you eaten yet?" he asked.

Emily swallowed, looking at the half-decimated artichoke. "Yes, I have."

"How about dessert? Are you up for that? It's only six-thirty."

She looked at her watch. Indeed it was only six-thirty, so why did it seem like such an eternity since she'd seen Darin?

"Dessert would be great." She vowed she wouldn't mess things up this time, as she had at breakfast.

"I'll pick you up in ten minutes."

Emily threw her plate in the kitchen sink and rushed to her bedroom to find something to wear. She shunned all the floral dresses that seemed to announce her lifetime in the church and found a pair of jeans and a baggy red T-shirt. Looking at her reflection, she felt disappointed. The jeans hung on her, as if she feared getting something that actually fit her, and the T-shirt covered her too-big jeans, making her look like a red potato with legs.

"I'm afraid this is as wild as it gets," she said to the mirror. "Scarlett, I'm not."

She put on her pearl earrings. Darin wore a cross in his ear. She giggled. She was dating a man with an earring. *Take that, Mom. We could share earrings. Well, earring.*

Emily knew exactly what her mother would say, and she

didn't want to hear it. She already heard echoes of it in her mind. Fireman Mike had been so upstanding, a local hero who was handsome and a longtime believer. He was everything Nancy Jensen expected. Everything she'd wanted in a son-in-law. But there was no spark between Emily and Mike. She'd wanted there to be. It would have pleased her mother and helped both women to forget their tumultuous relationship.

God's will and true love proved stronger than Emily's desire to please everyone else. Mike had never made her heart thunder like this dangerous stranger. She wondered if this were her way of silently rebelling. If her brother could see her now. The thought brought a smile to her face.

"You'd love him, Kyle!" Emily looked toward the ceiling. "Just because Mom wouldn't."

Her doorbell rang, and Emily sprinted for the kitchen, rinsing her dish and disposing of the artichoke before answering the door. She sucked in a deep breath and opened the door. Then she forgot to breathe. Darin's sage green eyes smiled, and she could feel her stomach flipping.

"Hi," he winked.

"Hi."

"Is it too soon to see me again?"

Never, she thought. "No, I actually missed you. I wanted to apologize for my strange behavior this morning. I'm not usually so strange, but I had a trying morning. It seems to me you haven't seen my best side as yet."

Darin bit his lip and looked straight at her. The directness of his gaze almost knocked her over. "Then I'm not sure I could handle your best side. Because I like all the sides I've seen."

Emily thought about asking him in but wondered what he would think of her country decor. Did it make her look too simple? She closed the door behind her. Darin didn't need to see any more of her floral ways. "Where shall we go?"

"How about a coffeehouse downtown? I know a great one."

"I'd love that. How was your mom's house? Did you have a nice dinner?"

Darin snorted. "It was weird. Thanks for asking. Things aren't the same since I became a Christian. They don't talk to me the same. Maybe that's my fault, but it still makes dinner different." He shrugged. "I don't know. My mom and dad keep hoping I'll come back around. I think they'd rather have me driving sports cars and living the life I used to. At least they understood that. I was a rebel and they accepted that. But this," he held open his palms. "They don't understand this at all."

Emily surprised herself, but she took Darin's hand. "I'm sorry. I know what it's like to be different from your parents."

He grasped her hand back. "Do you mind if we walk to the coffee shop?"

"Not at all." *More time with him,* Emily thought.

"East Palo Alto is the only place I fit in. The church doesn't know what to make of me, my parents would just as soon disown my religious ways, and my old friends have nothing in common with me. Becoming a Christian can be a lonely place."

"Christians shouldn't judge," Emily said.

"Yeah, but what would your parents think of me?"

Emily looked away, unwilling to answer the question. She knew exactly what her parents would think of him. She was glad they'd retired out of town. She'd only have so long before a gossiping goose at church told her mother what she was up to. She could hear the whispers now: *I hate to be the one to tell you, but Emily is dating a boy with an earring. He's not the kind you'd approve of, Nancy. I think you might want to plan a visit.* Her parents would probably move back without a second glance.

She held Darin's hand a bit tighter. "Maybe being a missionary will change people's mind. Do you have to wear the earring?" It was a fair question.

Darin shook his head. "No, but I got my ear pierced the day I became a Christian. With this same cross. I did it myself." He shrugged. "It means something to me, kind of a symbol of my new birth."

"I guess you do have to wear it then."

"The EPA kids accept it. I'm moving there this weekend with a couple of guys from the Bayshore House—that's a local ministry."

Her eyes widened. "You're serious." She clutched her stomach, wishing the butterflies would disappear. Darin was going to live in the inner city. She felt a small shiver down her spine. She certainly wasn't meant to live in the ghetto with a man who wore an earring. That wasn't the life for her. Her parents wouldn't be the only ones to tell her that. She slipped her hand from Darin's and focused on the sidewalk in front of her. Maybe her desire to annoy her mother was far too strong. But when she looked into Darin's eyes, her heart thundered all over again and she sneaked her hand back into his. Sometimes the head and heart disagree. She'd heard that said before, and that it was time to rely on God in those times. *Well, God, here I am.*

four

The dim lighting of the coffee shop created a soothing ambiance. An elegant, antique table stood in the center of the room on big black and white tiles, with smaller laminate tables placed elsewhere in true hodgepodge form. A huge metal roaster that resembled a wood-burning stove lifted to the ceiling and provided the focal point of the room. The machine announced the freshness of the beans, but the rich coffee scent overwhelmed the senses.

Emily drew in a deep breath. "That smell is just heavenly. Even if you don't like coffee, you have to love that smell."

"If you think it smells good, wait until you taste it." Darin winked, but then his eyebrows furrowed. "You do drink coffee, don't you?"

She bit her lower lip. "I like the kind with excessive amounts of sugar and chocolate poured into it, topped with whipped cream, of course."

He squeezed her hand. "I know just the thing. What do you want for dessert?" Pointing to the refrigerated glass cabinet, he motioned for Emily to look over the delicacies. Pies and chocolate concoctions beckoned her, and she looked to Darin with expectant eyes. She couldn't have said which looked more appetizing, the desserts or Darin's warm gaze. She looked away to settle her soda-fizzling stomach.

The shop's patrons consisted of tattooed, pierced youths,

older couples reading papers, and everything in between. The sounds of a jazz clarinet filled the room, and Emily saw that, next to the roaster, a lone musician played his instrument. The coffeehouse was the kind of place Emily would never venture into alone. Once inside, though, she was mystified. The natural shyness within her evaporated. She wanted to talk to everyone and find out their story. How did they get here? What were they doing tomorrow? What were they typing on those laptops of theirs? So many people, so many questions. She looked at Darin in awe. She was braver with him, and she liked that feeling immensely.

"Emily? Did you decide?"

"Oh, yes, I'll have the chocolate decadence cake."

Darin ordered their death-by-chocolate desserts, and they found a small table in the corner. "I'm so glad you came out with me tonight. I don't usually ask people out at the last minute, but somehow I thought it might be okay. You seemed to be having the kind of day I did."

"I'm so glad you called," Emily said. "I'm not usually bold enough to venture out on Sunday night. Ever since we stopped having evening service, I feel a little paralyzed at home. I usually do last-minute lesson plans and watch a video, but I can't get it out of my mind that it's church night. Maybe I should find something to do on a laptop and come here," she laughed.

"It's sad about Sunday evening service though." Darin shrugged. "I guess in the Bay Area people just didn't show up, huh?"

"No, and I think it depressed Pastor. He took it as a personal failure. They tried doing communion on Sunday nights to get the members there, but it ended up that the members weren't taking communion, so they finally just stuck to church and Sunday school."

Darin stared at her. "You are so beautiful. Do you know your face just lights up when you talk about the church or teaching?"

"Well, since you prefaced that with my being beautiful, you could have added anything onto the end of that sentence. You know, 'You are beautiful, but your feet are the size of a large tanker.'"

Darin's eyes laughed, and he looked under their table at her shoes. "Well. . ."

She playfully slapped his hand. "Seriously, I see that joy in you when you talk about the boys in the city. How did you get started with them?"

"You probably don't want to know."

"Yes, I do."

"I did a talk on drinking and driving at the Bayshore House. That's how I met the guys and started teaching the Bible study. It just ballooned from there."

Emily felt weak. Maybe she didn't want to know after all. She thought about her mother's prejudices and how she might answer them. *He's a good friend of Fireman Mike's. They met in the gutter. Yeah, he was arrested for drunk driving, but that's in his past. Oh, the earring. That's just his way of announcing his form of Christianity, Mom. And he started college. He just didn't finish because of partying.* Emily thought about the verse on being a new creature in Christ and wondered if there were any further way she could test that Scripture with her mother.

Darin must have sensed her discomfort. "I'm sorry, Emily. My testimony is not for the faint of heart."

All hints of a smile faded from his face, and she felt horrible she'd stopped him. "Do you think I'm faint of heart?"

He cupped her hand with his own. "I think you're sheltered, Emily. And that's a beautiful place to be. I don't ever want to take that from you. Innocence is a precious commodity. Cherish it. I wish I had."

A waiter in a studded leather jacket placed their order on a counter and yelled it out for all the patrons to hear.

"Excuse me." Darin got up and Emily watched him as he crossed the room. Except for the shaved head and the earring, one might never know he'd led anything but a respectable life. She wondered if she might make him more presentable if meeting her parents should ever come to pass. She chastised herself immediately for trying to change who Darin was. She should be so lucky that he would want to meet her parents.

"How did you find this place?" she asked when he got back to the table.

"I used to come here when I was studying for my contractor's license."

"You can study with all this activity?"

Darin looked around. "What activity?"

She crossed her arms. "You are so much like my brother. It makes me laugh."

"Your brother? I didn't know you had a brother."

"I don't anymore. Not that I know of, anyway. He'll always be in my heart. He's gone on to live a different life."

"I'm so sorry." Darin sat back in his chair, visibly shaken by her words.

"Me too," Emily said. "He's the only one who ever really

understood who I was on the inside, but my mother and he never saw eye to eye, and unfortunately it just got to be too much for him."

Darin leaned forward, his eyes meeting hers with such an intensity Emily couldn't break from their power. "Who are you inside, Emily?" he asked. "You come across as 'what you see is what you get,' but I can tell by your interest in people that just isn't the case. Just by the fact that you showed up at that wedding when no one thought you had it in you. So who are you really? You're obviously stronger than you give yourself credit for."

Emily shoved a bite of cake in her mouth. That was a question for the ages. Since her brother Kyle left, she had no idea who she was anymore. For so long she was Kyle Jensen's little sister, and then for a while Fireman Mike's girlfriend, but now she was just Emily, first grade teacher. Was there any more depth than that? She prayed so, but she sure couldn't summon it up if it was there. Teaching school was important, but when she saw how the boys looked up to Darin, she wondered if she'd have a lifelong impact on any of her kids. Since most of them were from wealthy two-parent homes, the needs just weren't as obvious. Darin looked at her expectantly.

"I don't know as yet, but when I find out, you'll be the first to know." She hoped that ended the conversation. In truth she feared she was no deeper than a sidewalk puddle. That wasn't information one wanted to share with a missionary from the ghetto.

"Tell me about your brother. You said he was like me." Darin swigged his coffee.

Emily smiled at the thought. "He didn't like rules either.

Kyle lived by the spirit of the law, rather than the letter. And in our house that was a terrible thing because we dotted every 'i.' " She looked down at her cake. "How my heart grieved when that part of our family was torn away and only the rules were left. Nothing was ever the same." She felt a tear fall and quickly wiped it away with the back of her hand. "I'm sorry. Give me a forum and I blubber like a fool. I'm one of those commercial criers, I'm afraid. Today I'm even worse than usual."

Darin gazed at her gently. "How long ago did your brother leave?"

"It's been ten years now. It was his first year of college, and I was already lost with him being away." She stopped abruptly. "You didn't come out to coffee to hear me whine. Tell me about your ministry."

Darin paused. "Tomorrow night we're going to San Francisco to a crab dinner and a play."

Emily shook her head. "Tomorrow is Monday, a school night. You're taking the kids up to the city?"

Darin threw back his head and laughed. Emily loved how he did that, as though he relished joy and emanated it like a flashlight. He didn't seem to care if anyone looked at him or if his laughter was out of place. He just laughed.

"Emily, these kids are up until one A.M. regardless. They watch cable movies all night that aren't fit for adults, and I think a night in the city is much better than what they could be doing. The playwrights' association donated the tickets, and I got the meals donated. Want to come along? I can invite two more kids if you go. We'll take the Bayshore ministry van instead of my car."

"I don't know. Monday night usually means a lot of grading for me. That would be a bit irresponsible for me to take off to a play."

"Irresponsible or out-of-character?" His eyebrows arched.

"Both."

"Hey, D." A tattooed, leather-clad man holding a helmet stood over the table.

"Rich!" Darin stood and clasped the hand of this frightening person. "Meet Emily." He motioned toward her, and Emily swallowed hard before taking the hand of someone her mother would have warned her about. Rich was covered with tattoos, mostly of dragons and spiders. He even sported a black widow above his left eye.

"Hi," Emily forced.

"This guy," Rich said as he pointed toward Darin with his free hand, "this guy is such a trip. Do you know he base jumped in a parachute from El Capitan in Yosemite? Just like Bond in that one movie. Crazy, man. He was lucky to be alive when they arrested him. A sheer granite wall he could have blown into any second." Rich gave a low whistle of awe.

Emily tried to hide her shock, but she felt her eyes blinking rapidly. Darin had been arrested. Really arrested! Not for any pro-life rally or something she could identify with, but for parachuting off one of the highest peaks in California. Of course, there was also the drunk-driving matter. She wondered if she could possibly handle a life with such a man.

Every time she heard something new, she took a step back mentally. If he wasn't so much like Kyle, she probably wouldn't be interested. But Kyle had been the same way. Gallant, good-looking, and fearless. It was hard for Emily to ignore what kind of heart lurked beneath Darin's history, and her own heart beat rapidly at the sight of him.

"It's not as shocking as it seems, Emily." Darin explained about the arrest. "That was a long time ago. I was young and stupid."

"Oh yeah, he's a church boy now I hear. Not doing any of those crazy stunts anymore," Rich said.

Emily looked outside at the pink twilight sky. It was too late for her to walk home alone, but she felt the immediate desire to leave. It wasn't the jail stint, it was just that the more Emily learned about Darin's life, the more certain she knew she could never be a part of it. She wasn't a fun person by nature, and she didn't want Darin to know that the last chance she took was trying a new lesson plan. Kyle had found their mother's home too stifling. Would Darin find her the same way? If so, it was better to know now.

Suddenly she longed to get home, have a cup of chamomile tea, and go to bed. Sunday night outings were just reckless. If she furthered anything with Darin it seemed her whole life would be that way. Out of control—irresponsible and frightening.

"Rich, I'd sure like it if you'd come to church with me one day. Jumping into faith was more exhilarating than any base jump I ever did." Darin started an easy sell job to Rich. It wasn't forced.

Rich put up a palm. "Not me, Buddy. I ain't the church-going type."

"And I am?" Darin asked.

"Point taken." Rich laughed. "I'll tell you what. You come with me to Burning Man, and I'll come with you to church."

Emily watched Darin carefully. How far was he willing to go for this guy? Burning Man was a get-together of life's weirdos in the middle of the Nevada desert. From what Emily heard there was a lot of nudity and strange art and then at the end they ignited a man-shaped structure and screamed at it.

"No, I'll tell you what. You come to church with me first, and I'll go to Burning Man with you. How's that?"

Rich shook his head. "Always the negotiator. You're too fast for my blood, D."

Rich patted him on the back and Darin sat back down. "Let's get together one of these days. Don't be a stranger. Emily, it was nice to meet you. You're too good for this guy." He winked and walked away with his helmet and gloves.

Emily swallowed hard. "Would you go to that event? Burning Man, I mean."

"Not in a million years." Darin rubbed his chin. "Unless God called me to it to preach there. Think about how many lost people are there looking for answers. Thinking they're going to find it in some invisible spiritual vortex like in a science fiction movie. It makes my stomach sick to think about it. I've been too close to death to think the afterlife is something to mess with."

Emily felt trapped in her chair, wondering how she came to be with such a divergent man. Right now, he seemed like a different specie entirely. "You know, I'd really like to go home."

Darin ignored her plea. "Do you know what the life verse I've picked out for myself is?"

"Do I want to?" she asked.

He cleared his throat and continued. "When David danced

before the Lord, he humiliated himself in front of people. His wife Michal was mortified and told him so. David replied, 'I will become even more undignified than this.' That's my life's verse. If God is calling me to something, I'm not going to worry about what society thinks, Emily. I'm going to listen and be undignified if necessary."

Emily could hear her own heart thundering in her ears. "But what about church society? If your life isn't held up in esteem, how do you earn respect? Being undignified is hardly godly behavior."

"There's a difference between being undignified and being undignified to praise the Lord. Are you afraid I'd embarrass you?"

She looked him straight in the eye and almost lied, but the truth came tumbling out. "Yes, I am."

He winced, and Emily felt her harshness to the core. Poor Kyle. Now she knew what he must have felt like when Mom couldn't accept him for who he was.

"I'm sorry. David cried out to the Lord so many times when he was humiliated, when he was downtrodden and beaten. What makes you call on the Lord?"

This date. "Just because I haven't had all these wild experiences doesn't mean I don't know what it is to need the Lord. I have endured tragedy multiple times, and I'm still standing." Emily scooted her seat back. "I think we should go."

Darin reached for her sweater on the back of the chair, but she grabbed it first. "Emily, are you afraid of me?"

She let the question fall unanswered.

five

Once home, Emily dropped her purse and ran to answer the phone. "Hello," she said breathlessly. She was thankful for the ringing phone so that she and Darin didn't have an awkward good-bye at the door. He had just waved at her as she clumsily ran for the phone.

"Emily, where have you been? It's Sunday evening. Shouldn't you be doing your lesson plans?"

She sighed. "Mom, I was out with a friend." *What am I thinking? Why don't I just announce I had a date!*

"A friend? Where?"

"We just went for coffee. It was no big deal. It's eight-forty-five and I'm home, okay? It's no later than I might have been home from Sunday night service. I just went out for a little fellowship."

"Are you dating someone?" Her voice rose with anticipation.

"No, Mom. It's just a friend that I met at Mike's wedding."

Nancy Jensen clicked her tongue in disgust. "Oh, that wedding. Why on earth did you go to that? Isn't it humiliating enough that he married someone else? You have to go and announce to all my friends that he married someone else?"

"I like Mike, Mom, and I like Grace too. It would have been unkind for me to stay home. I want to support their marriage. Besides, everyone at church knows the story. It's not like I'm keeping any secrets. What kind of lesson would it have been for little Josh if I didn't go?"

Her mother clicked her tongue again, followed by a long exhale of breath. "Emily, you are never going to get married being everyone's buddy. Men need to think of you as a woman, not as a companion they'd take to the ball game. I wish your brother was still around. He'd find you a wonderful man to marry. You do know you're my only chance at grandchildren."

It pained Emily to hear her mother speak as though Kyle were dead, and as though she herself had nothing to do with his disappearance. When Kyle was home, her mother didn't like anyone he brought around. Now that he was gone, Kyle was remembered as the salvation for Emily's singleness.

"Mom, you didn't even like parenting. What's with the sudden urge for grandparenting?"

"That's not true! Where do you get such wicked ideas? Mildred said she saw you with some bald man. You're not dating an old man, are you? There are so many strange men around now. You've got to be careful."

"He's not bald. He shaved his head. It's kind of the style now. The youth pastor even did it."

"What? It's true then? Emily, that is not the style for Christians. That is the style for hoodlums. I thought you wanted to get married."

"I do want to get married, Mom."

"Then the first thing I would suggest is that you find a man who respects his hair."

Emily giggled. She couldn't help herself. Each time she tried to stop, she only giggled harder thinking about a man who respected his hair.

"What are you laughing at, young lady?"

"Mom," she said through laughter, "where does a man who respects his hair hang out? So I know where to look next time."

"At church. That church has twelve hundred members in it. There are single men there and most of them have hair."

"There's one less now since Mike and Grace got married." Now she was just being ornery, as her mother would say. But did any woman at thirty-two need to be reminded she wasn't married? "Besides, I met the bald guy at church."

"So you are dating him?"

"I didn't say that. I just said that I met this man at Mike's wedding."

"So he's a firefighter!" She emphasized the word firefighter as if Emily was about to be rescued from her spinsterhood.

"No. He's a landscape artist."

"A gardener? Oh, Emily, really! You're a teacher. Your father and I paid good money for your education."

Yes, he's a gardener, and he was involved in a drunk-driving accident where he totaled his car and met Mike as a firefighter. It took everything in Emily's will not to announce the earring or the base-jumping arrest. Kyle's defiance had taught her mother nothing, and Emily's certainly wouldn't change her mind either.

"I'm friends with the man, Mom. Do you remember that Oprah show you sent me on videotape? It said to keep my options open and not to date a man based on his credentials."

Her mother stammered, "I didn't mean—"

"How's Dad doing?"

"He's fine. Maybe you should move up here with us. There are good teaching jobs in Oregon. The San Francisco area is known for. . .well, you know what it's known for."

"I have a good teaching job and I like California. We have sunshine."

"With your brother gone now, you're our only hope for grandchildren."

"And that lowers the odds quite a bit, doesn't it?"

"What is that supposed to mean?"

"Mom, Kyle had that kind of personality. People were attracted to him. They wanted to be around his magnetic presence. I'm not like that and I never will be. I'm Emily Jensen, first grade teacher. Let's just be happy with that, okay? That I'm not serving time in a mental hospital somewhere."

"I never meant I didn't think it was possible for you to be married. You're a beautiful, talented young woman. Surely. . . never mind. I suppose you're tired of hearing from me tonight. You always respected your brother's opinion. Do you think things will go anywhere with the gardener?"

"Tomorrow night we're taking a group of teens to San Francisco for a crab feast and a play." Emily surprised herself as much as her mother.

"To the city? On a school night?"

Help! I've become my mother. That's exactly what I said to him. "Darin says the kids stay up late regardless, so he's taking some of them to an African-American playhouse. They are doing a reprisal of the Brer Rabbit folk tales. I'll have to leave right when school gets out tomorrow."

"You're not going to lose your job for this, are you? First, you're out Sunday night and now you're talking about leaving right after school. I don't want to tell you how to run your life, but it's sounding reckless."

Emily thought about the endless school nights of planning and how her social life had always taken a backseat to her job. Even her summers were filled with summer school and committees. "Yes, it probably does sound reckless, but I've given my life to teaching. They can give me two nights that should be mine, anyway."

"Does anyone know this man who can vouch for him? It sounds a bit dangerous to head into San Francisco with someone you barely know."

"Pastor Fredericks vouches for him," Emily said with satisfaction. "Mom, I'll call you Tuesday night. I need to call Darin and firm up plans."

"Very well, but have your cell phone on so I can reach you if necessary."

"I will for everything except the play, Mom. I love you."

"We love you too, Dear. I'll be praying God brings you the man of your heart. And that he has hair!"

"Thank you." Emily rolled her eyes. "Tell Dad I love him too, and I'll see you both at Christmas. I'm planning to drive up there."

"We may see you before then. Your father and I just might show up on your doorstep for a surprise visit soon, so keep the furniture dusted," she mock-threatened. "Bye, Honey."

Emily hung up the phone and stared at it for a minute. Before she lost her mettle, she dialed Darin's number hoping he wasn't home yet. It was the first time she'd ever called a man, and it didn't feel right. He answered on the second ring. Emily gnawed on her lip before gaining the courage to speak.

"Darin, it's Emily."

"Emily!" He sounded pleased to hear from her, and she meditated on that for a moment. When had anyone been glad to hear from her within the last year?

"Darin, you said you could take two more kids with you if I went to San Francisco tomorrow."

"Yes! Tell me you're coming." His enthusiasm made her smile. How could anyone say no after that?

"I'm coming. I'll drive home right after school and meet you at the Bayshore House. I've tutored there before so I know where it is."

"No, Emily. I don't want you there at night. I don't even want your car there. I'll pick you up before we get the van. Okay?"

"That would be great."

"I'll see you about four. And Emily?"

"Yeah?"

"Thanks so much for calling. I'm thrilled you're coming. It will make the whole night that much better."

"Bye, Darin." She drew in a deep breath. Darin made her feel important, just like her brother Kyle always did. There was a gift in that ability.

❧

Darin hung up the phone and raised a fist to the sky. "Yes! Thank You, Lord! She doesn't hate me."

He scanned the room of his apartment; emptiness filled the place. Now that most of his belongings were boxed up and ready to move, he wondered if he were doing the right thing. Moving into the Bayshore House seemed like a great idea a week ago. Now he wondered. Emily was everything he wanted in a woman, but she obviously wouldn't be willing to live in the ghetto should their relationship continue. Would any woman worth having be willing to live there? He shook the thought. He had to rely on God for that.

Thinking back to their uncomfortable silence all the way home from the coffeehouse, he probably didn't need to worry about Emily and a future. She'd made it pretty clear that his past nixed him as a candidate for marriage after Rich's discussion of his arrest. It would probably nullify him with any woman worth her salt. He may have become a new creature, but the old one was still there lurking for other Christians to see like a scarlet letter upon his chest.

Images of Angel floated through his mind. There was a time when a beautiful woman like Angel was all he expected, all he could have hoped for. But now he wanted so much more. He wanted a woman that he was proud of on his arm, a woman whose heart highlighted her beauty. Not a woman who would flaunt it at a football game for any old geezer to gawk over. His whole definition had changed, and for that alone he was deeply grateful.

Darin ignored the moving box mess and went to his Bible. He needed confirmation, not questions. When he opened his Bible, a picture of the boys from EPA fell out, and Darin grinned. Those boys needed him. Was there any more confirmation necessary? Wanting Emily was one thing, but it wasn't enough. He knew the boys were God's will. He had no idea if Emily was anything more than a fierce desire. Angel had tugged his heart that way once too, and look how wrong that turned out to be.

"Hey!" Jack, Darin's roommate of four years, slammed the door. "Where you been? At your mom's this whole time?"

"Nah, I went out with a woman from church."

"Hope she's fine-looking, because Angel called while you were gone. She said she had some things of yours she wanted to return."

Darin sighed. "She's trying out for the Raiderettes. That's her big news."

Jack raised his eyebrows. "Is she now? I wish my dates looked as good as your castoffs."

Darin didn't know what to say to that. He remembered the day when all that mattered to him was how many men stared in awe at his date. It sickened him now to think how shallow he'd been. He was still a man, of course. He wanted a woman to be beautiful, but not in the same, showy way. Now he wanted a beautiful woman like Emily, whose dark hair and bright eyes shone with inner beauty. Emily didn't slather on makeup or cover up all her flaws professionally the way Angel did. There was an honesty to her beauty that stirred him like no woman had before her. Emily would give everything to the man she finally loved. How he wanted to be that man. He turned to face his roommate.

"Angel looks good on the outside, but you want more than that. Trust me."

"I'm not saying I want to get married or anything. I'm not looking for Mrs. Right. Just Miss Right Now." Jack laughed in his crude way, and Darin knew it was God's blessing that they were parting as roommates. Too much of Darin's past was tied up into this apartment, and Jack would never see the difference in him if he didn't do something drastic. Like move to EPA to work with troubled youths.

"I'm going out tomorrow night. I've met someone, and if

you meet her I'd really appreciate it if you didn't ramble on about Angel."

Jack cackled. "I'm no stooge. Since when do I ramble on about ex-girlfriends when the new one is in the house?"

"This isn't a girlfriend. This is something I take very seriously." He looked at Jack in frustration. "Never mind. Jack, have you noticed anything different about me in the past two years?"

"After your accident you mean? Before or after the conversion?"

"After."

"Yeah, you never date. Angel was the last woman I ever saw you with, and she didn't last too long. You're not going completely choirboy on me, are you? It's like this religion thing scared away the chicks. That's enough to scare me away. Have you put a curse on this apartment or something? It seems like forever since either one of us had a date."

Darin rolled his eyes. "If you read what the Word has to say about how we treat women, how we as men are responsible for how we treat women, you'd flee from this horrible broken life you lead." He hated giving sermons, but Jack wasn't listening anyway. Darin could say whatever he wanted.

"Hey, at least I've had a few dates lately. It's not like I'm going to take advice from you."

Darin dropped his head and shook it back and forth. "I'm praying for you, Dude." If he wanted confirmation, he had it and then some. These young kids he worked with still had a chance to lead their lives with conviction. He prayed God would show them how through him. Tomorrow night, he'd get to show them how to treat a date. He smiled at the reminder. Hope lived on. But definitely not in this apartment—after two years, Darin was tired of casting pearls before swine.

six

On Monday afternoon, after a long day of landscaping at a luxury home site, Darin showered and slapped some aftershave on his face. He hadn't been this excited for a date since. . .well, he couldn't remember ever being this excited about a date. He checked his watch again, and time seemed to lumber. Only ten more minutes and he could leave to pick up Emily. The phone rang.

"Hello, Darin speaking."

"Darin, it's Mike. How are you doing?"

Darin gulped back his emotion. The unwritten guy rule was that you didn't date ex-girlfriends of buddies. Did Mike know he was seeing Emily? Would Mike offer his blessings? Or think Darin's history was too dark for the likes of Emily Jensen. "Doing great. How was the honeymoon?"

"The honeymoon was fantastic. Fastest two days we ever spent, but Josh has school, you know. Carmel was incredible. You ever been there?"

"Yeah. My boss sent me for a bonus last year. Heavenly place, but it lacks a little something when you're alone."

"I can see that. Listen, we're going to take a smashed-up car over to Los Altos high school next week, and I was wondering if you'd be willing to talk about your experience."

Darin paused for a moment. He'd never hesitated to talk about his accident before, since it led to such a radical life change, but now he wondered. What would Emily think of him in her school district? If everyone knew she was dating a former drunk would that stop her? He hesitated.

"I don't know, Mike. Things are sort of busy right now. I'm working with the kids at Bayshore, getting ready to move and—" He let his voice trail off.

"I completely understand. Fortunately, we have a cache of speakers we can use. I just thought of you because of your testimony. Anytime we can work God into the program, we like that when someone gives proper credit for their life. I've got another guy who killed a high school student, but he has a hard time in the high schools for obvious reasons."

Darin's heart raced. All those kids, all of them thinking they were invincible, just like he used to think. "Of course I can do it."

"I didn't mean to guilt you into it." Mike laughed.

"Mike, I'm seeing Emily Jensen tonight. I met her this weekend at your wedding," Darin blurted.

"No kidding? Well, I'll be. You and Emily. Hey, Grace!" The phone became muffled. "Darin Black is seeing Emily Jensen tonight."

"That's wonderful!" Grace said from the background. "Josh would be so excited," she said, referring to her son.

"Don't tell Josh!" Darin said. "Emily's world has been so sheltered. I'm a bit worried about what she'll think of me being on the drunk-driving speakers' tour, you know? Do you think that will bother her?"

Mike paused for a long time. "It shouldn't matter what she thinks. I've never seen you care about what anyone thinks when it comes to sharing who you are. Besides, I think you should give Emily a little credit. She may come off as shallow sometimes, but still waters run deep, as they say. Emily's got a lot of heartache in her past. God has really grown her faith."

"Yes, she told me about her brother."

"Her brother, oh, right, that. Emily's a great gal, Darin. I hope things work out for the two of you."

"Just let me know the time on that talk, okay?"

"Will do. Grace and I will pray for you and Emily. I'm really happy to hear you're seeing her. She's a wonderful woman."

"I heard that!" Grace called out in mock jealousy.

"But of course not as wonderful as my wife," Mike said through laughter.

Darin heard a bit of wrestling with the phone, and Grace came on the other end. "I'm kidding, you know. I think Emily is just tops. Anyone who can teach kids all week long and find the energy to do Sunday school each week has to have sainthood written all over her. Grab her up, Darin!"

"Thanks, Grace. You looked stunning on your wedding day, and you can tell that lug I said so. He doesn't deserve you. Listen, I'm running late. I'll see you later." Darin dropped the phone back into its cradle and checked his tie, which hung crooked. He tried to fix the knot quickly and then grabbed his keys.

He dashed out the door, got into his car and drove the familiar route to Emily's house. Once there, Darin asked God to be with them all evening. He prayed for safety and bonding between the kids and Emily, and most of all for a fun time in San Francisco. He felt like he was going to his high school prom. For some reason, Emily felt more important than just a standard date. There was something about her eyes. In them, Darin saw a multitude of emotions, and somehow he felt God was actually pointing to her, saying, *This is the one.*

Emily opened the door and looked radiant. Her skin glowed clean and pink. She appeared not a day over twenty-two, and he almost thought he was robbing the cradle. Her dark hair framed her face and highlighted her striking eyes. Emily Jensen was a sight to behold. Rather than a simple floral dress, she wore a long pantsuit with a fitted jacket that cinched her small waist and strappy heels to match. Although she didn't show an inch of skin, other than her feet, Darin thought she was sexier than any woman he'd ever laid eyes upon.

He took her hand. "You look absolutely gorgeous."

She smiled and tossed his hand away. "My brother used to tell me that. I didn't buy it from him either." She winked at him and picked up her purse.

He watched her for a moment, not relinquishing his direct gaze. Could she possibly be for real? Didn't she have any idea what her smile could do to a man? Melt him in his tracks, that's what. And leave him a pathetic puddle on the porch. His heart thumped wildly, and he wondered if he would have noticed Emily's quiet beauty before his conversion.

"I don't care if you're buying it or not, Miss Jensen. You are gorgeous! Do you have a coat? It will be cold up there tonight."

Emily laughed. "I grew up in the Bay Area. I know about

San Francisco nights. Brrr." She pretended to shiver then grabbed a coat. Darin took it from her and laid it over his arm, offering her the other one.

"You ready to meet the kids?"

"How many of them are going?"

"Well, eight are signed up. How many actually go depends on how many show up, and that could be none. I've learned not to depend too greatly on the kids."

"None?"

"One thing I've learned about working in EPA is that time means nothing. It's a very arbitrary thing, the clock."

Emily laughed. "You got those boys to church on time yesterday."

"Only because I went to their house, and honked very early in the morning. That bugged their mothers, so they were out in a flash. There's an old saying, if Mama ain't happy, ain't nobody happy. And Mama's sleep after a long week of working two jobs is pretty important."

"You're kidding me. You honked outside the house?"

"Like I said, I've learned a bit in the last year. Today they have to come to me though. The tickets will be waiting at the door, and they'll give them away to someone else if the boys don't come."

"How did you get the restaurant to donate the meals?"

"I called and asked them. It's criminal that these boys should live so close to Fisherman's Wharf and never have eaten crab or San Franciscan sourdough. I told the manager that, and he agreed. I also told him we'd put an ad in the church bulletin for people who can afford the dinner. They usually say no, but once in awhile. . ."

"I can hardly wait! I love crab season. I've been dreaming about it all day."

Once they arrived at the Bayshore House, Darin saw a few kids milling out front. "It looks like a few of them showed up."

Emily squinted to look at the boys. "These are all new kids from yesterday."

"These kids all have grandmothers who make them go to their own church. Bless their hearts. The boys I brought yesterday are on their own most of the time, and their mothers appreciate the break on Sunday mornings. I only invited African-American kids tonight because this play is in a theatre that only does performances by black playwrights or plays that represent black history."

"How wonderful that they would think of those less fortunate kids in the audience."

"Think of it, I think that's part of the reason they do it. Maybe it will inspire one of these kids to write someday, and these kids have had so much tragedy, yet they still have an unbreakable hope at the same time."

Darin got out and opened Emily's door. The boys laughed at him for his chivalry. "Hey, what are you all laughing at? Do you have a date tonight?"

The boys broke into laughter again. "Nah, man, we're white."

Darin pulled out one of his pockets and translated. "White means poor. You only have the whites of your pockets. Emily, meet Reggie, Lonnie, and Sean."

All of the boys went beyond his expectations and shook Emily's hand. She asked each one about their school and took an active interest in their answers. He couldn't hide his pleasure. The exchange made him think he and Emily weren't too far apart. She loved kids. He loved kids. Surely, everything else could be sorted out.

With all the formalities out of the way, Darin looked at the boys. "Are you all that's coming?"

"Yeah. Danny and Rock had football practice, and Damien's grandma wouldn't let him go." At the last information all three boys broke into laughter. Rules were a comical thing in this town. And someone who adhered to them was absolute hilarity.

"All right then. We don't have to take the van. We can just take my car."

"Yeah! The grandpappy mobile," Reggie said to the amusement of his friends.

"The boys don't think my car is too cool."

"We liked the one he crashed. Not that we ever saw it." Sean crossed his arms. "But five liters of power and all those horses under the hood, and he has to go and total it before he gets here."

"You're lucky I'm here to talk about it. Now get in." Darin winked at Emily as he opened her door. "You don't mind riding in the grandpappy mobile, do you?"

Emily patted his Buick. "I'm a teacher in the San Francisco Bay Area. This is luxury to me. Everyone I know drives a compact of some sort, usually with a dent or two."

Darin thought he'd like to be in a compact tonight, with just the two of them, but his heart was full that she would come out with the boys. His joy felt complete.

Once in the car, the boys quickly commandeered his radio, and current rap tunes blared from the speakers. About halfway to the city, Reggie spoke up.

"Yo, we ain't eatin' none of that crab. Just sose you know."

Emily turned around and spoke for Darin, almost verbatim what he was thinking. "You boys can order a hamburger, but you have to at least try the crab. Otherwise, I'll have to tell the other guys you were too chicken." She shook her head and clicked her tongue. "That's gonna be embarrassing."

Darin could see Reggie's shock in the rearview mirror. "She's tough, huh?"

"Oh, man, that ain't right." Sean crossed his arms in mock disgust.

Once in San Francisco, Darin found parking fairly easily since it was Monday night. As he watched Emily and the boys climb from the car, his stomach twisted. This was how he wanted life to be. A beautiful woman and a ministry he loved. Life didn't get any better than this, and he hoped Emily saw it the same way.

seven

San Francisco's Fisherman's Wharf brought a certain excitement to Emily no matter how many times she visited. The steady tapping beat of the crab-crackers, the caw of gulls, and the sour yeasty smell of French bread mingled to create the perfect outdoor ambiance. The evening was remarkably warm, absent of fog, and both Alcatraz and Angel Island could be seen from shore. The red Golden Gate rose nobly in the background, and although Emily had lived her entire life in the vicinity, she marveled all over again. San Francisco was truly a beautiful city, one of the most beautiful in the world. She breathed in all the sights and sounds, noticing the boys did the same. Even in their "coolness" they were awed. Nature and manmade architecture coexisted magnificently in San Francisco, and Emily wondered if anyone could see it for the first time without a dropped jaw.

Reggie put his hands in his coat. A coat made for a remote winter in Alaska, not a fog-free Indian summer evening in San Francisco. But one never knew with this city. The fog could roll in anytime, and they'd all be freezing as if they were on a polar island. There was something about San Francisco cold that was unlike snow cold; it seeped into your body subtly, not like a biting frosty cold.

"San Francisco is the most beautiful city on earth." Emily finally let her thoughts loose.

Reggie bobbed his head up and down. "It's pretty decent."

Sean scanned the sailboats. "Not bad."

The rigging of the boats clanked joyously, and the salty air filled with colorful sights and sounds. The blue of the bay, the stark contrast of Angel Island, and the pristine white of boats in the harbor—it all delighted Emily's senses just as it had when she'd come with her parents as a child.

"Just being here makes me crave food. I always thought it was the chill of the evenings that made me hungry, but there's something Pavlovian about being here. It makes me want to eat."

Darin laughed and took her hand in his. She shivered at his touch. The boys all seemed to notice the motion but said nothing. Their respect for Darin gleamed obvious as they smiled among themselves.

"I think you're right. It's more palatable without the sea lions here. Their bark takes away some of my appetite." Darin laughed. "Okay, their smell doesn't do much for me either."

"They'll be back in January. We'd better eat while the season is right." Emily felt like a child in a wonderland. Being out on a Monday night, when she normally would have been correcting papers or working around the clock on lesson plans, overwhelmed her. She felt free.

Alioto's Restaurant had been on Fisherman's Wharf since Emily was a small child, and probably long before. She remembered her own parents forcing gooey clam chowder down her once a year. To this day she couldn't stand the stuff, but she knew it was a delicacy to most. As the rag-tag little group headed to the renowned restaurant, the setting brought warm emotions to the surface of her mind. Happy times—before her brother disappeared, before her mother had become so overwhelming.

"My mom and dad used to take me and my brother here at least once a year."

"Mine too," Darin said.

"While you all is strolling memory lane, we be hungry," Sean quipped in bad English.

Darin laughed. "Y'all ought to be strolling grammar lane."

"Yeah, yeah," Sean answered. "You date a teacher and we's supposed to talk like Shakespeare."

Emily bristled at the word usage but couldn't help her laughter, and she tried to put her teacher's voice to use. "Poor grammar makes people think you're stupid. And I've heard enough to know you're not stupid."

"Man, not in the hood it don't. We start talking like you, we get our—" Reggie snapped his mouth shut. "Never mind."

Emily listened to the banter with interest. She'd spent her whole life in the Bay Area, and she'd never known anyone from the "hood" as they called it. With a mixture of fascination and disbelief, she realized tonight was the first time she'd stepped out of her comfort zone and her own upscale city. Even if she was poorer than a church mouse while living there and educating the wealthy kids, she'd never know what it was like to be in the hood. Or so she hoped.

Her gaze traveled to Darin's muscular form, his set jaw. She knew she would be protected this evening. But how realistic was a date like this? And another? And another? Darin had his world, and she had hers. Barricaded and protected was the life she knew how to live. Darin lived his life without training wheels or brakes. She felt herself shiver.

Close to the restaurant, a homeless man shifted on the dock, and Emily jumped and clutched her chest. For a moment she thought she imagined the movement, but the shifting continued. His clothes were an ashen gray that blended into the salt-worn wood of the building. The man's stench was horrible. His brown beard was covered with bits of food, and Emily felt sick to her stomach. It was hard to tell where his beard ended and his face began, so gray in tone was he.

Reggie approached the man and Emily nearly pulled him back, but Reggie dwarfed the man. "Yo, man, you okay?" As the man rolled upwards, Reggie pulled back. "Whoa!" His nose twitched.

The man nodded that he was all right and started mumbling to himself. Why weren't people like this in proper facilities? Suddenly Emily felt alone in the bustling area. Everyone walked right past them, and she wondered why they weren't doing the same thing, moving on. Yes, they were Christians, but this man was beyond help—steeped in alcohol and his own world.

"You hungry, man?" Sean asked.

Darin just stood behind, taking it all in and not saying a word. Emily wanted to call the police. She kept her cell phone clutched tightly in her hand in case the man made a move, but she guessed he had some kind of right to be there. It was a public place, but he certainly was doing nothing for her appetite.

"Ch–change?" the man finally stammered. "You got any change?" He sat up when he noticed the group gathering around him, but his position looked precarious—as if he might fall at any moment.

"No, man, no change. You hungry?" Lonnie said.

"Yeah, I need money for food." The homeless man moved like a sea lion, bulky and slow. But when he moved, Emily automatically felt herself stepping backwards on the pier. The boys, however, stepped closer, and Darin still did nothing to stop them. He held up a palm, like he knew she was annoyed, but he wanted to see the scene played out. If they all ended up dead in the Bay, she wondered if he'd chalk that up to experience too. She'd been a teacher for too long to willingly allow kids to enter into danger.

"We ain't got no money, man. We'll get you some food if you's hungry."

The man just nodded slowly in resignation. Without checking with Darin first, Lonnie rushed across the street and dodged into a convenience store. Emily watched the whole thing in disbelief.

"You're just letting him go over there by himself?"

"He's 275 pounds! Who's going to mess with Lonnie?"

"He's a minor child. Alone in the city."

Darin looked at her. Then he looked deeper into her eyes, and the spirit of fire she carried for the moment left her like a torch drenched in water. Darin, though burly and broad in the shoulders, moved with the grace of a dancer. He stepped lightly toward her, his eyes gentle and concerned.

"Emily, you worry too much. Lonnie lives in East Palo Alto. Fisherman's Wharf has nothing on him. It's all right. I promise. I'm not going to let anything happen to the kids."

Emily felt her face flush red. "You're responsible to Lonnie's parents for his well-being tonight."

"I am concerned with his well-being, Emily, but God's

ultimately responsible for it. I can't let a man go hungry because of fear." Darin whispered loudly and with enough force that Emily's angst returned with a vengeance. She was not heartless, but who knew what this man hid under his filthy jacket? Darin pulled her aside, away from the two boys, who hovered over the homeless lump.

"Lonnie has a heart as big as the Pacific Ocean. The boys are hungry, they said so themselves, but they cared more about that man getting some dinner because they know they aren't that hungry. So I've got time for that." Darin's tone was that of an angry principal, and Emily felt the hairs on the back of her neck prickle in her defiance. But he continued. "Lonnie has been given nothing in this lifetime and yet still has time for good character. So, yes, I'm responsible to Lonnie's mother, and tonight I'll tell her, if she happens to be home at midnight, that her son is a quality human being. Despite her pathetic upbringing."

Emily wanted to crawl into a discarded crab shell. She felt the sting of tears, the threat of them spilling, but she refused to give way to them. He saw her only as coldhearted and icy, but she just wanted to protect the children. Why didn't Darin see that?

"I'll wait over by the restaurant."

Darin grasped her arm gently. "Emily, I don't want you hanging out in the city by yourself. You're safe with me. I promise." He looked at the boys. "You're all safe with me, and most importantly, you're safe with Jesus." He turned and looked at Emily. "What are you so scared of?"

Afraid of, she wanted to correct him. She was reminded that the beauty of San Francisco was much darker in the company of Darin Black. Her parents had each grasped one of her hands, lifting her in elation as they walked the pier. Now she stood beside a homeless man who obviously hadn't seen a bath in weeks. She waited on a linebacker-sized kid from the hood while he did his good deed, and everyone was just fine with the situation but her. She was not callous. She was cautious.

It wasn't that she didn't have a heart, but they had missions for this. She gave her old coats and blankets every year to the local shelters. That didn't mean she wanted to stand in trembling fear with a crazy man who talked to himself and didn't bathe. She wasn't heartless, she was savvy and level-headed. And right now she wished Darin was the same way.

She pushed a few tendrils of hair over her ears. "I shouldn't have come. I suppose that's what you're thinking right now. I'm sorry if I'm ruining your fun."

Darin grimaced, obviously not wanting to discuss this in front of the boys. He pulled her to the fence that protected them from the water below. "On the contrary. I'm ecstatic you're here with me, but I want you to believe in me, Emily. I wouldn't put you in danger, and I'm not going to let anyone hurt you." The dinging of the sailboats clanged more insistently as a gust of wind blew forth.

Let anyone hurt me. Like thieves came up and asked for permission. As Emily opened her mouth to speak, Lonnie came darting across the street, a small carton of milk and a hot dog foil in his hand. He gave the food to the homeless man.

"Here, man, it's hot. Be careful," Lonnie said as the man devoured half the hot dog in one bite.

He sat up and smiled broadly at the boy. "You thought I'd use the money for drink."

Lonnie nodded. "Yeah, man. You don't smell like you need more drink."

The homeless man laughed, and Emily saw his humanity for the first time. She swallowed hard and turned away, unwilling to face her emotions. Fine, so he was human. She still wished she were inside the restaurant away from the dark reminders of San Francisco's seedier side.

The man eliminated the rest of the hot dog and nodded. "Thank ya kindly, Kid."

"It ain't nothing, man," Lonnie said. "You'd do the same for me if you could."

With that, the three boys headed toward the restaurant, and Emily followed with Darin at her side. He smoothed his shaved head. "Those boys have hearts of gold, huh?"

She pursed her mouth shut for fear of saying what she felt. She'd imagined a night of romantic bliss, not a night in the depths of humanity learning some kind of valuable social lesson. This wasn't *A Christmas Carol*. She wasn't Scrooge.

"You know, Darin, I don't mean to be rude. But I was taught that people like that man back there were dangerous. I was taught it's quite inane to give them anything because they become dependent on handouts. Give a man a fish and all that." She tried to keep her voice down so the boys didn't hear her chastising Darin. "I don't know that you've taught the boys anything of value here. You could have placed them in a dangerous situation."

Darin looked at the boys in front of them and then halted his steps. "Emily, there's about one thousand pounds of us, and a homeless man in a heap on the dock. I guess I just fail to see the threat." He blinked, waiting for her answer.

"He could have had a gun," she suggested.

"He could have had a machete and a nine iron too."

Emily looked away. "Now you're just making fun of me."

Darin brushed the back of his hand along her cheek. "I am not making fun of you, Emily. You're right. I should have taken you on a proper date. I just wanted the boys to meet you, and I guess I got a little ahead of myself." He cupped her hand in his. "For tonight, I ask one thing. That you would trust me for just this evening. I know I'm not your standard fare when it comes to dating. I just can't help myself when I see someone down on their luck. It's like something in me clicks. Two years ago that was me in the gutter, and Fireman Mike rescued me for Jesus. I feel indebted every day and I want to repay." He clasped her hand tighter. "I don't know how to put my gratitude into words, and actions just never seem enough."

"But no one said anything to that man about Jesus."

Darin shook his head. "We were Jesus to that man today. That's more important than handing him a tract, Emily."

She had never encountered this in her lifetime in the church, and she squirmed in her uneasiness. She was a good Christian. She lived a good life and set a good example for her students. She left the gutter-gathering to others. Was it so wrong that she hadn't been called to evangelize? She bit back tears.

"A good tract is an important item."

"Not without relationship and prayer. Only God can make a tract come to life."

Emily checked her watch. It was going to be a long night. She wanted to live a bold faith, but it wasn't in her. Looking into Darin's misty green eyes, she didn't think it would ever be. It was just like a young writer aspiring to be the Hemingway of his generation. One only had so much capacity for learning. Part of it had to come from God.

eight

According to the car's dashboard, it was 11:47 P.M. when Emily arrived home. After they'd dropped the boys in EPA, the ride to her home was nearly silent, and she didn't know how to break it. She wished for something to say, something that might let Darin know she wasn't proud of her actions, but that she'd been frightened   nonetheless. His silence spoke volumes. This evening had been like trying to force a puzzle piece that didn't fit into the puzzle. Darin and she shared a strong attraction, but little else. She didn't share his vibrant outgoing personality, and she certainly didn't share his lack of fear.

Emily supposed she'd sounded callous, judgmental, and unconcerned for her fellow man. She might have felt guilty if she hadn't legitimately panicked. Her thoughts drifted away at the sight of her lighted front porch.

Darin turned off the car and faced her. His handsome face was lit by a lone streetlight, and when he turned toward her all ambiguity was gone. She wanted to forget the life he led. She wanted to follow Darin into the barrio and learn his ways, but she wasn't that type of person. She wasn't that type of Christian. Couldn't he see that? Some Christians were called to the mission field, and some were called to other pursuits, like children in the public school system.

Darin spoke, his voice forlorn. "I'm sorry, Emily. I really

am. I had hopes tonight would be different. I had dreams of dining you over the San Francisco Bay and gazing at the sunset and the Golden Gate Bridge with the kids learning how to treat a woman. I guess I'm not the romantic I imagine."

"But you wouldn't change what happened tonight?" Her tone sounded so angry and clipped. She felt ashamed and almost astonished that she'd chastised him as easily as she did. Like he was one of her students.

"Wouldn't you have done the same thing? That man was hungry," Darin said. She could see his eyes blinking rapidly under the street light. It was obvious he didn't understand her at all.

Emily sat up straight, trying to maintain a sense of decorum. "You know, we're just obviously called to different ministries." Sadness enveloped her as she spoke.

"We both love children," he said.

"But it's different. You work with children I don't understand and teenagers." She crossed her arms, but inside her heart withered a bit. She sounded remarkably like her mother. A woman who scared most children to the point they'd run from her at church. Would Emily grow old the same way? "I want to work where I'm comfortable."

Darin spoke quietly, reverently, and in a way that commanded attention. "You know, Emily, I run the risk of sounding judgmental here, but God didn't give you a spirit of fear. I don't know what you were so frightened of in San Francisco—that guy was an old man who needed something to eat. He obviously didn't have the strength to pursue us, much less the motive."

"No motive, you say? He's sleeping on the pier and you think he has no motive to steal? I don't think you're judgmental, Darin, I think you just live in a world that's far too trusting and naive. We're obviously called to different arenas." She shrugged as if none of it mattered, but her heart pounded. The clipped voice continued as if it had a will of its own. "No harm done, I suppose. Thank you for an interesting evening." She started to grasp the door handle but turned back. In her own way she was hoping Darin would stop her.

Darin clicked on the light in the car. "No, it's not okay. If you never see me again, that's your choice, but you can't live your life for Christ cowering behind the safety of your little created world, Emily. 'There is no fear in love.'" He quoted Scripture, which only infuriated her more. Yet, in some strange way, she felt softened. She actually envied Darin's self-assuredness. "You fear because you don't trust God."

Her stomach roiled. "What? I have trusted God my whole life. So my faith isn't bright like a newly lit candle as yours is, but mine burns constant and true. Yours may prove to be a flicker in time." Just as she said it, her hand flew to her mouth. Darin's demeanor sparkled bright with the Holy Spirit. She didn't know where her tears came from, but she started to cry. Guilt mounted and she had to face the truth, as ugly as it was. She controlled her world. God did not.

"The man was hungry," Darin said again, and this time Emily got it. She swallowed her tears as if they were an acceptance of something hateful. Something she didn't want to own, yet must. "I didn't help him and he was hungry," she repeated.

"Whatever you do for the least of these. . ."

"I do for Jesus." How many times had she taught that Sunday school lesson?

And then, as if showing her he forgave her, he added, "I'd like to bring you home for dinner to my parents' house. You're nothing like what they imagine I'd be interested in, and I admit I'm kind of excited to show you off."

"I don't imagine I'm anyone you would be interested in." Emily forced a laugh. She didn't want to put herself through this again. Her world may have been simple, but it was predictable and safe. She could learn to trust God more on her own terms.

"You're wrong there. I know this isn't easy, you and me. But I feel it with everything in my being that we're meant to do something great together." He paused before adding, "Are you busy Thursday night?"

"I have choir practice. For the kids' Christmas musical at church."

"Friday night then? Do you want to have dinner with me again? Or do you think of me as some kind of project." He looked away when he asked, as if he was nervous for her answer.

Why did he care? It was obvious nothing serious could ever come from this awkward relationship. Why didn't Darin just move on? Like her brother Kyle had done, like Mike had done, and like all the men in between.

A crash suddenly broke the silence, and Emily felt shards of glass hit her arm. The passenger window had been broken, and drops of blood trickled down her arm. Darin lit from the car like a rocket, and she saw him chasing a man down her darkened street.

Emily looked to her feet in utter amazement. There was no purse at her ankles, only broken glass everywhere. When her mind stopped reeling, she heard herself call out to Jesus, begging for Darin's safety. She punched her cell phone and dialed 911, but her fingers shook and she had to dial it three times before getting it right.

It was all so fresh, she could barely tell the operator what had happened.

"There was a man," she gasped.

"Where is the man?" the operator asked.

"Ran down the street. Darin chased him."

"Who's Darin, Ma'am?"

"My friend." Emily exhaled deeply. "My purse is gone."

"I need your location, Ma'am."

She hadn't even given her address. She did so and then blurted, "When will you be here?"

"We have an officer in the neighborhood. They'll be there soon. Which way did your friend head?"

"North, toward Cuesta Drive."

"Help is on the way. Are you hurt?"

Emily clutched her arm. She had a small cut. "I'm bleeding a little on my arm. Nothing serious."

She lost all sense of self and just wanted to know Darin was safe.

O Lord, bring him back to me.

GET OUT OF THE CAR!

Emily heard the voice as clear as day but had no idea where it came from. She didn't question it. Once out of the vehicle, she looked around, unsure what she should do next. She stood there in her apartment driveway, as if waiting for some miracle voice to tell her what to do, but nothing came. Nothing happened.

In her shortness of breath, Emily started to run in the direction Darin had gone. Soon she had a steady gait going, and she screamed out, "Darin!"

No one answered her.

She screamed again, "Darin, answer me!"

Again, only silence met her shaken voice. At the corner, she saw Darin's coat crumpled in a heap. She swooped to pick it up and stood for a moment, calling his name desperately. He moaned, and she saw him lying on his side.

"Darin!" Emily grasped his shoulders and turned him over. The dim streetlight lit his face, and she saw a gash in his forehead. "Darin, no! What happened?"

"Pipe," he mumbled. He reached to touch his forehead, but Emily grabbed his hand.

"No, don't touch it. Help will be here soon." The wail of sirens pierced through the late night, and she ran into the street to stop the policeman. She waved him down, standing directly in his path. To her relief, the vehicle slowed down.

"Help me! A man is hurt."

The policeman radioed for help and climbed out of the squad car, leaving it running. He bent over Darin's frame, shining a flashlight into those brilliant eyes that first caught her attention. Now the sight of those eyes, under a canopy of pain, wrenched her heart. She could still hear her heart beating, not from her own fear, but for Darin.

If he wasn't okay, she'd never forgive herself. Her cold words came back to haunt her, and she tried to force her own voice away, but the echo kept coming. *He could have had a knife.*

"Is he going to be okay?" Emily heard herself ask the officer.

"Paramedic's on the way. He's got a concussion. Has he been conscious at all since you saw this?"

"He spoke to me. He said the word pipe."

"Do you know if he's had a concussion before?"

"I think so. He was in a bad car accident once."

The officer nodded. "How'd this happen?"

Emily pointed behind her. "I live up the street. Darin and I were in the car and someone broke in for my purse." Her voice trembled in her disbelief. She lived in a solid neighborhood with upstanding people. She'd just come from the inner city. "How could they have known where my purse was? Tell me he's going to be okay."

"Did you have a light on in the car?"

"Yes," Emily shrugged, not understanding the question.

"People on drugs are often attracted to light, like a moth to the flame. Do you know if the assailant hurt himself on the window?"

"I never even saw him until Darin chased him, then he was just a shadow." She let out a small sob.

"Ma'am, you need to calm down. He's been hit hard, but we'll get him help just as soon as we can. It's probably just a simple concussion and he'll be back with us soon. I'm going to need a statement from you."

Emily shook her head. "No, I'm going to the hospital. I need to be there for Darin. I wouldn't feed the hungry."

The officer looked at her cockeyed but didn't question her babbling. "I'll get you there as soon as I have your statement. Do you want to find the guy who did this?"

"No—I mean I don't care. I just want Darin to be okay."

The paramedics arrived and went straight for Darin. Emily stood idly wondering what she should do. She wanted to help, but when she stepped forward the officer held her back. Seeing bold, muscular Darin lying helpless in a crumpled heap on the lawn brought chills to her spine. For her purse, he'd ended up this way. She thought about the $12 cash she carried and wanted to cry out. For $12 and a few credit cards, someone had done this.

"Ma'am, please. I just need to get a statement from you."

Emily turned toward the officer and nodded. Silently she prayed, undone by the night's irony. She'd survived the San Francisco Embarcadero and Theatre District, and the inner city of East Palo Alto, only to be mugged in her own safe-haven neighborhood. Someone had a wicked sense of humor and she tried to force the thought from her head that it was God.

Emily told the police all she could remember, but it was so very little. All, except the voice that propelled her from the car. She didn't think hearing voices made for a very good witness. She heard Darin moan again, and she felt the sound to the soles of her feet. *There is no fear in love.* Shockingly, with all she'd witnessed tonight, she felt no fear. She knew with everything in her being that Darin would be fine. With amazing clarity, she realized she trembled from the cold. For once in her life, she wasn't in her comfort zone and she wasn't afraid. Her eyes narrowed at the sight of her pained friend. She felt only anger now. Life wasn't fair and it really should be.

nine

Peacefully, Emily sat among the city's transients. She didn't even know Los Altos, home of the rich, had transients, but there they sat—smelling of liquor and in desperate need of clipping shears. She drew in deep breaths and let them out fully, the way she'd been taught at Pilates exercise class. Although she felt peace, she was still felt thankful for the metal detector at the door. She feared sharp objects within the vicinity of these men. She focused on watching the cable news show and reading day-old newspapers in the Emergency Room waiting room.

Emily called Darin's parents, after guessing with the local phone book. Luckily, they were listed. His mother didn't sound pleased to hear from her, but who could blame the woman? It was the middle of the night, and she brought bad news. Hardly the way to ingratiate oneself into the family.

Not long after, an older couple rushed into the waiting room, heading straight for the triage nurse. Emily knew that must be them.

"Someone called us. Our son is here, Darin Black." The woman wore full makeup with dyed black hair and had the same striking green eyes as her son. Smile lines didn't frame her eyes the way they did Darin's. Rather, she had one deep crease in the center of her forehead. Emily got up to greet them.

"Only one of you may go in at a time," the nurse droned.

The mother exhaled. "Why? We're both his parents."

"Because those are the rules." The triage nurse crossed her arms, making it obvious the subject wasn't up for discussion.

"That's fine. We'll wait for his fiancée to get here. She's parking the car and she'll want to see him.

Emily sat back down, her eyes darting about the room. She knew Darin didn't have a fiancée but couldn't imagine why his mother would make one up. It was the middle of the night. Where would they find an imaginary fiancée? Had Darin lied to her?

"Only family members allowed," the triage nurse repeated. "His fiancée doesn't count without a marriage license. See security when you're ready and decide which of you will go in." With that, the nurse sliced the window shut and went back to her paperwork.

The mother cursed, and Emily winced. Darin's mother was nothing like she imagined. Darin emanated joy while his mother seemed angry at the world. His father just looked conquered, as if any means to speak up for himself had long since disappeared. His chin hung low and he sat down in a chair, obviously waiting for his wife to make a decision for them both.

"I'll go in first," Mrs. Black stated.

Mr. Black acquiesced with a nod of his head.

Emily went toward the couple. "Excuse me, I'm Emily Jensen. I was with Darin tonight when he was hit. I mean, I was with him in the car before he chased the man."

Mrs. Black looked Emily up and down. She felt the scrutinizing glare and squared her shoulders against the laser-sharp stare. "What was he doing with you?"

"We went to the city tonight with some of his kids from East Palo Alto."

"This happened in the ghetto? I should have known." Mrs. Black couldn't hide her disgust at the mention of EPA. Her face puckered like a prune. With shame, Emily thought she and Mrs. Black weren't as far apart as she would have hoped.

"No, actually it happened on my street. In Los Altos."

"Los Altos? You must be kidding me. You're the one who called then?"

Emily nodded.

"Who are you?"

"I'm Emily Jensen," she repeated. "I teach first grade in Los Altos. I met your son at a wedding in our church."

Mrs. Black sighed loudly. "My son is not the type to go to church, Missy. Whatever he told you, it's temporary. He's always into one phase or another, and right now I'm afraid he's into the tortured sinner role." She lowered her voice. "His future bride will be here any minute, and I don't think she'll like finding you here. But I do appreciate your phone call and concern. That was very sweet of you." She paused before adding with a smile. "Very Christian of you." Then she motioned with her hand for Emily to leave. "Thank you again."

Emily stumbled over her words, but confidence filled her. "Mrs. Black, your son is not engaged." She said the words gently, hoping that she was not offending. Mrs. Black had enough on her mind, but Emily hated to see Darin's reputation tainted by his mother's beliefs. "I feel quite sure our pastor would know about it if Darin was betrothed, and he was the one who set us up. I don't want anything from your son,

Ma'am, and I really want to stay until he's out. I feel responsible since he was at my home."

Mrs. Black's eyebrows shot up. *Oh, that didn't sound good! It implied something definitely not good*, Emily thought.

"My son is lying in there on a hospital bed, and I can guarantee you who he'll want to see when he wakes up. Darin and Angel have a long history together, Dear, and I know you wouldn't want to stand in the way of that. Please just do him a favor and leave, being the good Christian girl I know you are."

For a moment Emily's legs gave way, and she turned toward the door before turning around again. "I beg your pardon, Mrs. Black, I didn't mean to be disrespectful, I only meant—" She stopped. What good would it do to argue with an upset mother? "I'll be leaving. Please be sure and let Darin know I was here, and that I'll call him tomorrow."

"Of course we will." The way she said it in staccato implied a curse word.

She nodded at Mrs. Black, for Mr. Black never said a thing. He watched the television as if it had a laser beam pointed directly at him. As Emily was exiting, a young woman was entering. The woman demanded attention. Even in the middle of the night, she wore full makeup and her hair shone in dark silky waves. The contrast between her olive skin and red lipstick lit her complexion as though she were on stage. Even the drunks looked up.

"Angel!" Mrs. Black gripped the young woman's hands in her own, and Emily faltered. Angel, as she was called, looked like someone from a lingerie catalog. Her small frame was graced with long legs and a tiny waist. There was a synthetic appearance to Angel, and Emily felt weak. She stood in the electronic doorway, causing the doors to partially close and then open again.

"Can you step out of the door please?" the triage nurse yelled from her guillotine window. The Blacks and Angel all turned toward her. Emily, against her better judgment, stepped back into the waiting room.

With all eyes upon her, she stepped forward and thrust out her hand to the gorgeous brunette. "Hello there. I'm Emily Jensen. I was with Darin tonight when he was hurt."

Angel stammered and didn't hold out a hand. Emily dropped her own and shrugged to let Angel know she wasn't intimidated. But of course she was. Angel possessed the kind of beauty that rendered men speechless, and she couldn't help but compare herself. She tried to remember Darin's words about fear. Being intimidated was not allowing God to work within her.

"Why was Darin with you?" Angel's eyes held contempt. She let her slender fingers trace down her long hair.

"We were up in San Francisco tonight with some of the kids he works with."

Angel's eyes lingered on Emily's comparatively shapeless figure, and subconsciously Emily crossed her hands over her waist, suddenly sure that Darin and she were futile. Darin garnered the kind of attention that frightened Emily. He possessed an invisible charm that emanated from him like a high beam while she was the exact opposite: the mousy teacher that people tended to forget in the corner.

Out of the corner of her eye, Emily saw the triage nurse smiled coyly and cock her head sweetly. She saw why almost immediately. Darin's broad frame stood by the triage door, he smiled and thanked her for the prompt attention. She giggled and bit her lip. Darin's face was pale, but his eyes shone with vitality.

"What kids?" Mrs. Black asked Emily since she didn't see Darin.

"From my ministry." Darin winked at Emily. He came toward her and put his arms around her.

"Darin," she breathed. "You're all right."

Darin closed his grasp around her. "They just wanted to observe me. Make sure I didn't have a complex concussion. I was ripe for one after my accident last year. Did you know once you get one, you're more likely to get another?" Darin looked at his family over Emily's shoulder. "If I'd known I'd get all this attention, I might have done worse to myself. It's kind of like attending my own funeral. Do you all want to say something nice about me now? I'll wait."

Mrs. Black came forward and pulled Darin toward her. She roughly moved his chin. "Let me see your eyes."

"Well, I still can't drive tonight if that's what you're worried about. Emily will take me home. My car's at her place, although the window's broken out."

"Angel came to drive you home," Mrs. Black said with authority. Emily could feel her fingers starting to tingle. Darin had all the charm in the world, but this was clearly a bad situation. He had a concussion and was expected to make a choice in the middle of the night. A choice that would clearly have reverberating results. Silently, she prayed that she could handle whatever his choice was.

"Angel, thank you." Darin reached for Angel's hand and

shook it, never relinquishing his grip from Emily's waist. "It really was nice of you to think of me."

Angel looked as if she might catch fire. Her ample chest heaved and her teeth remained clenched. She smiled through them tightly. "It was your mother that thought of you. I was asleep in the middle of fantastic dreams when she called. I thought with our history I owed you a visit."

"You'd better get your rest. Aren't your cheerleading try-outs coming up?"

A tinge of jealousy shot through Emily. If the game of chess had cheerleaders, she still wouldn't be qualified. With her small stature and conservative clothes, she looked more like Angel's mother. Certainly not her rival. She squeezed Darin's hand tighter for support. He turned his eyes to hers, and she swallowed at the strength in their gaze. He wore a bandage on his right temple, but it did nothing to diminish his good looks. It only made him appear more masculine.

"Darin, you can stop your games now. We all know a relationship with the schoolmarm isn't going to last." Angel looked down at Emily. "I'm sorry, Honey, but he's not your type. Darin likes the wild side of life." She tossed her head back and laughed. "Do you remember when you drove us to Nevada on your Harley?" And to Emily, "This religious thing will pass, and you'll have an untamable stallion on your hands. I'm doing you both a favor. Darin can come home with me."

Emily saw Darin's jaw twitch, but he laughed lightly. "No one needed more grace than me, Emily. Angel can attest to that fact. So can my mother. But you know where my heart is now."

Emily forgot their audience. "I needed more grace than I ever knew. I found that out tonight on the pier. At least you knew it. I was living in ignorant bliss as a Pharisee."

"A what?" The corner of Angel's mouth lifted. "You two want to speak English here? For those of us not up on the current religion-speak of the day."

Darin kept his eyes glued to Emily but spoke to Angel, " 'For it is by grace you have been saved, through faith—and this not from yourselves, it is the gift of God—not by works so that no one can boast.' "

"Whatever," Angel said, putting up a palm in front of them. "Darin, when you're ready to come back to the real world, call me." She looked at Mrs. Black. "He's a freak now. When he's away from the moonies, call me."

"Son!" Mrs. Black said as Angel walked out the door. "Don't do this. You're not going to marry that little wallflower."

Emily felt the first sting of tears.

Darin's eyes thinned. "I'll marry whomever I please. Considering that Emily and I haven't completed our first date alone yet—"

"Look at her!" Mrs. Black motioned toward Angel's departing frame. "She's the most beautiful girl you've ever dated. She's sweet and I can teach her to cook. You've only got so much time. Soon every man who sees her on national television will want her, and you can't exactly compete with a professional football player."

Darin reached down and kissed his mother. "I'm not trying to compete with a football player. I'll call you first thing in the morning, Mom."

"Should you sleep after your concussion?"

"The doctor said I'm fine. Dad, Mom, thank you for coming all the way down here."

Mr. Black grunted. Mrs. Black pulled Darin from Emily's side. "This is serious."

"There's more to beauty than the outside, Mom." Darin whispered the words, but they were like a dagger to Emily's soul.

He didn't think she was beautiful on the outside, and her insides felt ripped apart.

❧

Emily grew quiet, and her swirling thoughts blossomed into full-fledged emotions. She didn't look like Angel. While she was comfortable with that fact, she wasn't comfortable with being thought beautiful only on the inside. Yes, the Bible may have called for that in Proverbs 31, but she'd read Song of Solomon too, and she wanted the man she admired to desire her physically. It wasn't that she wanted to look like Angel, a woman who gave herself freely to anyone who would look; she wanted Darin to understand that just because she didn't flaunt her figure did not mean she didn't have one.

"What's the matter, Emily? You haven't said anything since we left the hospital, and we're almost home." Darin pressed his hand to the bandage on his forehead.

"Nothing." Emily clamped her mouth tight in a straight line.

"I hope my mother didn't say anything to upset you."

"Nope."

"Angel?"

"Nope."

"Then what it is, Emily? Am I just too much trouble for you? I bet you've never had to work this hard a day in your life, huh?" He forced a laugh.

No, actually she hadn't had to work this hard. Dealing with Darin was like dealing with a foreign student in her classroom. She knew there was so much he was capable of, but they spoke different languages. God wouldn't make romance this difficult. Would He? Their evening date had stretched into the wee hours of the morning, and neither of them needed more drama right now.

"You've given me a lot to think about. Living in fear is not living at all."

"Wow, you got all that tonight?"

Emily nodded. "You would have been proud of me if you'd seen how I handled myself." *When your mother came on the scene.*

"I am proud of you. You came out with me on a Monday night, and look, I stretched it into Tuesday and you're still here. I'm impressed by that."

"Your mother wants you to marry that girl."

Darin laughed. "I bet your mother wants you to marry someone too. Is it going to happen?"

Emily felt her stomach flutter. "The man my mother wanted? He got married to Grace on Friday, so it's not going to happen. Alas, I think her hopes for grandchildren are quickly dwindling."

Darin grabbed her hand and squeezed. She felt an electric pulse shoot down to her toes. "I certainly hope not. You'll make beautiful babies, Emily."

ten

The week passed like molasses, and Emily hadn't heard from Darin. Not a phone call. Not a note. Nothing. Countless times she'd picked up the phone to call him, only to have her mother's voice ring in her ear. "Good girls do not call men." So she'd place the phone back into its cradle and correct more papers or create another lesson plan. At this rate, she'd be ready for school in January.

She tried to think the best. She figured Darin was busy with his move, and she tried not to worry that the blow to his head had erased her from his mind. Even calling him to check on his head felt pushy, so she avoided it. Tomorrow was Sunday, and she was certain she'd see him at church. Then she could put her fears to rest. She climbed into bed and prayed to God that if He were to take Darin from her life forever, He would also take away any desires she had for a family.

Although she'd known Darin such a short time, she could already picture him as a father. What a good father he'd be. She'd also seen the possibility of her wearing white down an aisle—although her mother, and his, would heartily protest. Maybe that was part of the romance of it all. The forbidden love affair. She hoped that's all it was because it was humiliating to wait for the absent phone call.

Once at church, Emily kept one eye on her Sunday school curriculum and one eye on the doorway, hoping Darin would bring the boys from EPA back to church. But service ended and there was no sign of Darin or the boys. Despondent, she put her things into a bag and headed toward her car. Stepping out of the sanctuary, she saw Angel. Her stomach knotted. Was she here with Darin? *Please, God, no.*

Emily forced her chin to the sky and tried to walk right past Angel, who was much better covered than the last time they'd met. Her conservative shirt showed off her pretty facial features, and Emily couldn't help but wonder why Angel would force everyone's eyes toward her chest by dressing suggestively. Seeing the pain in Angel's eyes, she walked up to her.

"Hi, Angel."

"Darin's not here?" She blinked back tears.

Emily felt her knotted stomach clench tighter. "I haven't seen him this morning. Was he supposed to meet you?"

"No," Angel answered quietly. "I had just hoped to find him here. I don't know where he lives now that he's moved into the ghetto. I didn't want to call his mother. She gets so excited that we're getting back together. I figured you'd know where he was. Actually, I figured he'd be here."

"Did you try calling him?" She couldn't help the hope in her voice. She wanted to know desperately if everything were okay. *Ugh.* She wished her mother had told her sometimes it was okay to call men. She might not be living this turmoil if she'd known there was a time to break the rules, but rule breaking was just not in her character. And no matter how many times she'd pressed the buttons, she couldn't bring herself to push the final number.

Angel continued. "Yes, I called him. His old roommate

doesn't know the new number. He asked for mine to give it to Darin when he called, but I just didn't trust him enough to give it to him. Darin knows my number."

Emily forced herself to breathe. "I haven't heard from him since that night in the hospital, so I'm afraid I can't help you." She felt so broken, admitting that Darin hadn't called her. Standing next to this striking brunette, Emily was ready to get herself to a nunnery—though she wasn't Catholic and she didn't exactly know what nuns did. She was chaste and loved the Lord, and she was never getting married. So she probably qualified for the nunnery—except for the Catholic part.

Angel looked truly worried. Her dark brown eyes glistened, and she wiped her reddened nose. "So you don't know where he is either? Or you don't want to tell me?"

Emily smiled. "I don't know where he is." She wanted to feel for Angel, this lost ship looking so desperately for an anchor, but she felt her own pain too deeply, her own loss of Darin's whereabouts too keenly. Jealously was an ugly emotion, an ungodly emotion, but she felt it just the same.

"I didn't make it as a Raiderette," Angel sniffed. "I don't know why I feel the need to tell Darin about the failure, but I do. So if you know where he is, I wish you'd tell me."

"I'm sorry." Emily's voice sounded cool, though she hadn't meant it to. What did one say to a woman who didn't make the professional cheerleading team? If Angel wanted to compare failures, Emily had been to three weddings in the last two years for men she'd once dated. That probably qualified in the loser hall of fame. "But God must have different plans for you, Angel. Better plans."

The woman's hard expression melted but returned almost

as quickly as it disappeared. "Look, I know Darin is seeing you, and I'm sorry, but I can't help but feel you don't have the right to him. Darin and I were meant to be together. I knew that the day I met him, long before he got into this religious thing. Whenever something happens, good or bad, we call each other." She stopped and licked her lips. "There's some comfort in him that I just don't believe he'll ever have with someone else. So, excuse my rudeness, but I feel you're in our way, and I think you should just do the Christian thing and bow out gracefully."

Bow out. Emily didn't know she'd ever bowed in. "It might be the Holy Spirit," she said. "The Holy Spirit is a very attractive presence. Have you always felt this way about Darin? Or just in the last two years?"

"Are you crazy?" Angel's full red lips parted in disbelief. "I've seen him during these last two years. What does that tell you?"

"That you two should either get back together or not see one another. We've got more in common than you want to admit. I think we've both been enamored with Darin's natural charm and his fiery presence of the Holy Spirit."

"Whatever."

"Clearly, something else is more important than either one of us. I haven't heard from him this week either." Emily shrugged her shoulders, trying to feel camaraderie with this pinup model.

"Do you have a point, or are you just messing with my mind?"

"My brother Kyle was like Darin. He had friends galore and girls calling at all hours of the night, and I really knew

Kyle. I never saw him do a thing to really encourage the girls, except talk with his natural charm. But still they followed like he was the Pied Piper himself. Maybe we're both following Darin the same way."

"We?" Angel laughed.

"Yes, I say we. I'm not immune to him." Emily crossed her arms around her Bible. "And he's not immune to me either, Angel. I may not be as beautiful as you, but Darin and I share a strong connection."

Angel's chin quivered, but she didn't answer.

"I can tell you one thing," Emily continued. "Darin knows the Lord, and he won't marry someone who doesn't." She offered one of the church student Bibles that were available for taking to Angel. "Start in the Book of John." Angel kept her hands tightly clenched.

"You know, it's just like you Christians to talk in code. I have no idea what that means, to 'know the Lord,' and quite frankly it creeps me out. I came here to find Darin, not to get some pious speech from some freak. Darin will marry me. Just as soon as he gets away from people like you. You all remind me of those aliens in *Toy Story* who worshipped The Claw."

Emily winced at Angel's harsh words. She closed her eyes and prayed for peace, trying to see Angel for the hurt child she was within, but the taunts of her own childhood haunted her. While the other girls had cool jeans and stylish haircuts, Emily wore long dresses and had stringy hair. She was a freak, and the words still cut like a knife.

Pastor Fredericks emerged from the church, and Emily saw her escape.

"Pastor!" she called. "I'd like you to meet Angel. She's a friend of Darin Black's and is looking for him. Maybe you could help her." *I certainly can't.*

Angel looked like a trapped animal, but she smiled and held out a hand. Obviously, Darin's pastor might have some answers, and she wasn't willing to risk rudeness with a man of the cloth.

"Excuse me," Emily said. "It was nice to see you again, Angel."

This was one rejection she hadn't been prepared for. Darin had pursued her, Darin had asked her out. He'd actually said she would make cute babies—and now where was he? Long gone, like all the other men in her life. Only this one had left without a trace.

"Emily!" Grace waved at her from across the courtyard. The mere sight of Grace forced tears, as she was just another reminder that Emily had run another one off.

"Hi," Emily said, emotionless.

"What's the matter?"

"I'm short, among other things."

"What?" Grace's brow furrowed. Emily couldn't help but wonder what it was like to go through life looking like Grace. Or Angel. She was the kind of woman you walked right on by. She didn't grab attention or make men do double takes. She just was. Emily sighed.

"Emily, did you hear me?" Grace's voice jolted her.

"Do you see the leggy brunette over there? She's looking for Darin." *Just like you came looking for Mike.*

"I see her. So?" Grace shrugged.

"So it's time for a change, I think. I'll start with churches.

I've been going to this one my whole life, and I'm quickly becoming known as a black widow, the kind of woman who swallows up men in her evil lair and spits them out a mere shell of themselves."

Grace's eyes twinkled. "You're kidding me, right? You do not possibly believe you have any such reputation. Everyone loves you here. You can't just leave because of what a few nasty people think. No one who knows you thinks anything like that. Darin called Mike and he sounded very excited about you two seeing each other. You don't know that this woman means anything to him. You and Darin are still dating, right?"

Emily looked over toward Angel. "Not anymore apparently. I suppose I'll be attending his wedding next."

Grace was silent for a moment. "I'm sorry, Emily. I'm sorry things happened the way they did with Mike. I never meant to get in between you and him."

Emily shook her head, annoyed that she couldn't keep her negativity to herself.

"No, Grace. I didn't mean it that way. You know I didn't mean it that way. God made you two for each other. I'm not thinking I got left behind, trust me. I'm just feeling sorry for myself today, a bit self-conscious. You were just the closest victim. I mean friend." She smiled slightly.

"I don't think you should be thinking about any major changes because of Darin. There is a place for you at this church, regardless of what happens with him."

The words of comfort didn't really register. She was like a broken record that her parents played when she was small, stuck in the same annoying groove. The only way to fix that was to knock the needle past the difficult spot, and that's what Emily felt she needed to do.

"My parents are up in Oregon. They've been trying to get me to move. I'm thinking now I might go. I could get a new job, a cute little place of my own—I could afford it up there, you know."

"You're going to change everything because of Darin?"

Emily laughed. "No, not because of Darin, just because I'm questioning what kind of person I have become. Do you see Angel over there? Well, Grace, she is at the exact same point you were when you met Mike. She doesn't know Jesus, doesn't seem to want to, and I can't see her broken heart. I don't like her because she's so hateful, but how would I expect her to act? I haven't learned the lesson, and I think I need to get over this wall before I'll ever be worthy of living for God. I know I'm redeemed, but I want to live that way. I saw you as a dangerous viper, a single mother who made an unforgivable mistake. I was totally wrong about you. I'm not the judge and jury, and yet I keep thinking that about other people."

"I think you're being hard on yourself, Emily. You were one of the first people to welcome me into this church. I'll admit you were cold when I started, but you were the first one to warm up to me, really. The first one to understand Josh was more than just a youthful mistake."

"I want to start again. I want to be a better Christian, a bolder Christian, and I don't know how to do that here. Looking at you is just a reminder of my failure."

"I'm shocked! I really feel you were responsible for changing Josh's heart—which eventually changed mine."

Emily blinked rapidly. "Really?"

"Ask Mike if you don't believe me. Emily, you were vital in Josh's life. You told him about God when you could have been fired for doing so. If you hadn't planted the seeds for Josh, you wouldn't have planted them for me either. Don't ever deny God's power in you."

Emily pulled her hair into a makeshift ponytail, blinking back tears.

"Angel over there is a beautiful woman, but she's not half the woman you are. Not even close," Grace said.

"You know, I've heard that my whole life. You're a sweet girl, Emily. You're such a doll, Emily. What would the kids do without you, Emily? But I'm selfish underneath it all. Just once I want to hear *I love you, Emily*—and the man is there for me one week after he says it. Just once I want him to stick around, not walk off with someone who looks like you, Grace."

Grace had tears in her eyes. "The right man won't walk off. I promise you. And God will never leave you." She looked over at Angel. "She's very beautiful, but her heart is not. I can tell that from the scowl she wears. Look, Emily, there's Darin now. He didn't abandon you."

Emily's head snapped up and she saw Darin walking toward her. His expression changed when he noticed Angel standing beside Pastor Fredericks. Whomever he chose was his choice. She swallowed hard and waited. He hesitated, standing on the curb for a moment before offering a warm smile and a nod to Emily. His long legs then strode purposefully toward Angel.

She tried to smile at Grace. "I guess we have our answer, don't we?"

"Don't think that. We don't know what is going on, Emily. It's unusual for Angel to be here. I'm sure Darin's just concerned."

"Excuse me." Emily jogged toward her car and climbed inside before her tears fell freely.

eleven

Darin looked at Emily and the knot in his stomach tightened. He could see the pain in her eyes. He wanted to run and gather her into an embrace. But then he saw Angel. Angel talking to a pastor. It was a sight he never thought he'd see, and his feet stood planted. He hesitated only a moment before he walked toward Angel and Pastor Fredericks. From the corner of his sight, he saw Emily run, but he had to rely on God to fix that. *Father, please be with her.*

"Angel, is everything okay?"

"Darin!" She burrowed herself into Darin's chest. He unwittingly wrapped his arms around her and questioned Pastor Fredericks with his expression.

"What happened?"

"Your friend Angel was just telling me she didn't get a job she was counting on," Pastor Fredericks said. "We were talking about God's will and disappointments."

"You didn't make the cheerleading team."

Angel shook her head and sniffled. Her dark brown eyes were rimmed with red, and her nose had a touch of pink at the tip. She'd clearly been crying heavily for some time.

"Do you want to get some lunch and talk about it?" Darin asked.

Angel sniffled again and nodded.

"Darin, can I speak with you first?" Pastor Fredericks said, his forehead wrinkled.

"Sure. Angel, here are my keys. I'll meet you in my car. It's right over there." Darin watched her walk away defeated, and his heart pained him. "What is it, Pastor?"

Pastor Fredericks rubbed his chin thoughtfully. "I wanted to warn you about 'missionary dating' and how that applies to Angel."

"I beg your pardon?" Darin had heard the term, but he hardly saw how it applied to them.

"A beautiful woman in trouble is a temptation that I'd be very cautious about, Darin. Angel is a nice girl, and I understand your friendship goes back a ways, but don't let her neediness translate into the fact that only you can help her. Pray for her."

"I'm not thinking I'm the only person." He stood a bit taller. He didn't like where this conversation was headed. He wasn't some mealy-mouthed wimp who couldn't handle talking to an ex-girlfriend. What was Pastor thinking? That Darin would be so overcome with lust he couldn't control himself? The notion angered him. He had a responsibility to share Christ with her.

As if Pastor read Darin's mind, he continued. "Maybe you should think about asking God to raise someone else up for Angel. Sometimes in our attempts to do God's will, we end up buckling under the pressure of the outside world."

"Pastor, I appreciate your concern, but I'm not sure you understand about Angel and me. We have a long history together, and I'm not interested in her that way."

"I just watched Emily Jensen run from here, and she

looked upset to me. You can't straddle this fence, Darin. You've got to make a choice. Women don't like to share. Remember Rachel and Leah?"

"I'm not going to make a choice between Angel's salvation and dating Emily, if that's what you're saying. Emily will understand, she has a heart for people. You worry too much, Pastor." Darin winked. "I wouldn't do anything to hurt Emily."

Pastor Fredericks crossed his arms. "I'm not worried about Emily being hurt so much as I am about you getting in too deep. Emily has a lot of friends, and she can handle whatever comes her way. She won't wither away into a shell; that's not what I'm saying."

Darin shook his head. "I've been friends with Angel for two years. I'm not going to just abandon her when she's hurting and I've got an opening for the gospel."

"I'm not asking you to abandon her. I'm just asking you to be accountable. Being alone with a woman in that condition is a warning sign. That's all I'm saying."

Darin started to laugh again but saw that Pastor Fredericks was dead serious. He wasn't interested in Angel that way, and without his mother there prodding things along, he felt completely safe.

"Don't look at Angel as a project for faith, but as a woman God loves and will search for."

Emily's car exited the parking lot, and Darin hated the choices set before him. He knew that Pastor meant well, but he was obviously overreacting. Angel needed him right now, and what kind of Christian would he be if he just walked away?

"Thanks for the advice. Angel is waiting. I'll pray on it tonight."

Pastor lifted his brows. "I'd pray on it before I got to the car if I were you." Nodding his head, he turned his attention to another congregation member and left Darin alone.

Rather than praying, Darin mumbled all the way to the car about Emily. What was going on? Didn't she understand how rare it was for Angel to show up at a church? Couldn't Emily see the blatant cry for help?

"Women!" Darin grumbled. "There's just no making them happy." He got to his car and saw that Angel had shed her conservative sweater. He swallowed hard at the sight of the tight pink T-shirt that hugged her curves and forced his eyes away.

"What took you so long?" she asked in a voice completely free of melancholy.

"Pastor had something to discuss with me." He cleared his throat. "You know, Angel, why don't we go talk with Pastor right now?"

Her tears started again. "I don't want to talk about my failures with a man I never met before. I came to my friend." The way she emphasized friend made his skin crawl, and suddenly he wished he'd heeded his pastor's advice.

"Angel, look. I don't want to hurt you, and I need you to know that God cares for you more than you can possibly imagine. But I can't make this hurt go away. I can't make things any better for you."

"No, you won't make it better. There was a time when you cared for me, and now that you're religious and I'm not, you are just abandoning me."

"That's not true, Angel. I'm here, aren't I?"

"Only in body. Not in spirit." She moved closer to him. "But if that's all you're willing to part with."

Darin backed away and hit his head on the window. "Ouch!" He rubbed his head, feeling like a child running from a scary stranger. "Angel, you're just trying to tick me off, and it isn't going to work."

"Then why don't you go find Miss Goody Two Shoes? Clearly, she's all you can handle anyway."

Darin's heart caught in his throat. What was he doing? Angel didn't want anything to do with the Lord? She wanted to find a way into Darin's mind, and this was her way. The only way she knew. He looked at her with sympathy but knew he was not the man who could make a difference in her life. He was only endangering his. But a real man proved himself with self-control.

"Angel, you're right. I'm not enough man for you. I suggest you find one, preferably with the name of Jesus. I'll meet with you and Pastor Fredericks anytime. But I won't meet with you alone again. I'm going to find Emily and salvage what we have left. I love her, Angel. Nothing you do or say will change that. She's the one I want."

Angel let out a string of curses. "It's not enough that I have to lose my cheerleading status? You pick today to tell me we're through? You are coldhearted, Darin Black. Coldhearted. God has done nothing for you. You've only become more selfish and more heartless. You think only of yourself. As always."

Darin stared at her pert nose and angry eyes. "I'm sorry you feel that way. If you'll excuse me, my girlfriend is waiting for me."

"You wish she was. I saw her peel out of the parking lot. I may not have you, but you don't have her either." She crossed her arms, and Darin could see she had no intention of getting out. He grabbed his keys and left the car without another word.

Outside the church, he saw Mike Kingston, the fireman who'd saved his life. "Mike!"

"Hey, Darin. What are you up to?"

"I need a ride to Emily's. Can you give me one?"

Grace came up beside her husband. "I don't think Emily wants to see you right now."

"You talked to her?" Darin asked.

"You walked over to your ex instead of Emily. Bad move. It's been a week since you've called her. I'd say you're in a bit of a pickle, Darin. We women do not like coming in second with a man we're interested in. Worse yet, to come in second to another woman, that's lethal."

"If that ain't the truth," Mike added, shaking his head.

Darin felt as though he were getting everything he deserved. "I didn't call her because I did that drunk-driving speech this week, and I didn't want her to have to explain to her colleagues that she knew me."

Grace gave him a look of disgust. "Why don't you let Emily make that choice? She's a big girl, and she doesn't need you deciding what's best for her."

Mike laughed. "You've heard about a woman scorned? What you haven't heard is how they stick together."

"I'm a terrible boyfriend. I admit that. This morning I had planned to make everything up to her, but one of my kids had a fire in his grandmother's house last week. I had to make sure everything was settled with them."

Mike kept shaking his head. "Darin. Darin. You have great excuses, but I can tell you from experience, they are all useless with a woman."

Grace slapped her husband on the shoulder. "We women just want to know what's going on. Emily just assumed you weren't seeing each other anymore. Lack of communication is deadly, you know."

"She said she didn't think we were seeing each other anymore?"

"It's been a week, Darin. What is she supposed to think?"

"We'll give you a ride, but then you're on your own. Don't say we didn't warn you." Mike laughed.

"Where's Josh?" Darin asked.

"He's with his grandparents this weekend. Come on." Mike led the way to his truck, and they all piled into the front seat. The ride to Emily's was quiet. All the way there Darin rehearsed what he'd say to the woman he loved.

At Emily's house, he felt confident enough to wave Mike and Grace off. The last thing he needed was an audience for his groveling session. He rang the doorbell and waited. There was no answer. Sighing, he sat at the edge of her porch and waited for her return. *Mental note: Do not teach inner city boys about romance. It is not my gift.*

He watched each car pass expectantly and glanced at his watch. He'd wait one hour, and if she hadn't shown up yet perhaps it wasn't meant to be. He kept thinking about Emily. About her enthusiastic smile that turned to a frown when he walked over to Angel. What could he have been thinking? Maybe he had more head injury than he gave himself credit for. As he mentally beat himself up, Emily pulled into the driveway. She got out of her car and looked at Darin. Then she walked around to the trunk and pulled out a few grocery bags.

It was worse than he thought. She felt like a stranger to him now.

twelve

Emily blinked several times. Someone was sitting on her small porch. A big someone who resembled Darin, but she knew better. Darin was with Angel now. Still, her stomach flip-flopped at the possibility. She'd hoped Darin would be different. That he would tell her the truth rather than let her find out the hard way. The way she'd found out her brother was gone. Hope sprang eternal, but Emily thought of her pastor's words about mental illness: to do the same thing twice and expect a different result. What did three or four times make her? How she wished Kyle were still around to translate man-speak for her. Squaring her shoulders, she pledged that she was done playing the welcome mat and prayed for strength.

I will not fall victim to my feelings. I will not fall victim to my feelings. I will be strong.

It was high time Emily started spending more time with God, rather than constantly looking for a man. That was a wasted effort. If God wanted her to be married, He could just have the guy knock on her door and sweep her away. Since that wasn't likely to happen, she unloaded her groceries from the trunk.

"Hi," Darin said, his voice tentative. He took the groceries from her. She nodded at him and unlocked her front door.

"So it is you. How's Angel?" she asked, unable to help herself.

"She's upset," Darin said, as though Emily really cared. It was hard to be overly concerned for the other woman. No matter how godly one was.

"Good, so am I. Thanks for asking."

"Emily."

She took the groceries back from him and put them down inside the foyer, then turned toward him. "Darin, I never asked to get involved with you. You were the one who kept asking me out. If you weren't over Angel, you shouldn't have strung me along."

With annoyance, she realized a tear had fallen. Darin wiped it away with his thumb.

Clearly, he hadn't expected her to stand up for herself. Doormat Emily never did, after all. He could just ask Mike Kingston if he didn't believe it for himself. But those days were over. She was far too old to be every man's buddy. If she ever hoped to be taken seriously as a woman, she needed to stop wasting her time with men who wanted a companion at baseball games. She needed to trust in God, not herself.

"I wasn't stringing you along." Darin's jaw set. "Angel lost out to the other women for cheerleader. She was upset."

"Well, then, that changes everything. Look, lest you think I'm jealous or envious or any of those things that bring out the green-eyed monster—maybe I am, but that's not all I am. I'm just sick of being taken for granted by men. I thought we had something between us. At least enough where you would give me the common courtesy of letting me know if you were really with her. I know that's what your family wants."

"Angel—"

"Angel had nothing to do with why you didn't call me all week when you said you would."

"No, she didn't."

Emily felt the first sting of tears in her nose. For someone who never had a serious boyfriend, her batting average with men was horrible. She supposed dashed expectations were to blame. It served her right for having any. Relying on people would get you nowhere, that's what her brother Kyle always said. Only God, Kyle used to say. That was an easy thing to say, but not easy to live. Relationships were a vital part of living.

"Emily, are you willing to hear why I didn't call you?"

Was she?

"I don't know. Is it going to hurt me? Because if it is I think I'd rather remain blissfully ignorant for now."

He put his arm around her and led her to the sofa. "Do you remember Lonnie? The kid we took to San Francisco?"

"Of course I do. Big as a house with a heart to match." She grinned thinking about the boy.

"That's him. Did you read about the arson fire in EPA in the paper? That was his grandmother's house. Lonnie's cousin suffered smoke inhalation and has been in Stanford Children's Hospital all week. I've been staying with Lonnie and his cousins, so his grandmother could be at the hospital. I wanted to call you, but every time I did someone needed me for something. And I figured that's why God called me there, so that was my priority at the time." He shook his head. "Looking at your face today, I don't know that it was the right choice."

He touched her face with his palm, and she saw the honesty in his eyes.

"How is Lonnie's cousin?"

"He's fine now. It was touch and go for the first couple of days." Darin shook his head again. "Emily, I'm terrible at this. I'm trying to court you, the way a good Christian man should court a woman, but I'm at a loss. You're not like any of the women I've dated before."

"I've noticed."

"Angel doesn't mean anything to me. It's just that I can't stand to abandon someone who is so obviously looking for faith."

"Is she looking for faith, Darin? If she is, that's God's job. Not yours."

Darin raked his fingers through his hair. "No, she's not looking for faith. At least not yet. Pastor told me the same thing, that it was God's job, not mine. But I admit I'm struggling with the idea. What if no one else comes along? What if her time comes and she doesn't get it? As it is, she's a death sentence waiting to happen."

It was a good question. What indeed? She wondered if God weren't preparing a special ministry for her. Bringing women to God so her old boyfriends could marry them. Now there was a harsh thought. At the same time, the eternal life of a soul was so much more important than her pride. Or her marriage dreams.

"I'll talk with her. Do you want me to talk to her?" Emily asked.

"I would if you don't mind." Darin got up from the sofa. "Let me help you put these groceries away."

Emily watched him stride toward the kitchen carrying the brown bags as if they were cotton balls. He embraced a humility she didn't understand.

He came back into the living room, and Emily's heart clenched. He was so good-looking, inside and out, and her feelings toward him were like nothing she'd ever felt for any other man. There was an invisible attachment to him, a chain that held her heart and told her Darin was a gift from God. But how could he be? Everything about him was wrong. He lived in the ghetto. His parents hated her. Her parents would hate him! He wore an earring. Was it really worth going on? God didn't want her to bring all these differences to a marriage. Marriage was hard enough, wasn't it?

"Are you going to help me with the groceries?" His eyebrows rose. "Or are you going to make me do it myself as penance?"

Emily laughed. "I should make you do it. It's quite attractive to watch a man work in the kitchen. Go ahead."

He walked toward her and picked her up as easily as one of the grocery bags. "I'll give you working in the kitchen." The two of them collapsed on the couch in a flurry of laughter. And then Emily's smile died as Darin's eyes met her own. "I'm through playing around, Emily. I took you for granted because I thought you knew my heart. I won't make that mistake again. Grace read me the riot act."

His expression moved her heart. She loved this man. How

could that be true so quickly? But she knew. "You haven't even kissed me."

"I can change that." Darin grasped her chin gently and pulled her toward him. They melted into a soft kiss, and Emily couldn't imagine ever kissing another man.

The doorbell broke the moment. They separated like two teenagers caught in a high school hallway.

"The door," Emily said.

Darin broke into laughter. "It is the door."

"I'm stating the obvious."

"You are." He pushed her up from the couch. "You should get the door."

She nodded and headed toward the door, but all she wanted to do was find her way back into Darin's arms. She smiled at Darin, searching his green eyes and forgetting what she was doing.

"The door," he reminded her.

"Oh, right." She opened the door, and her mouth dropped. "Mom! Dad!" Emily looked back at Darin, and all she could focus on was his shaved head. His earring.

Nancy Jensen stepped into the duplex while Emily's father waited on the stoop. "You've got a man here?"

Emily exhaled, trying to contain her own emotions of guilt. "Mom, Dad, this is Darin." Her dad, wearing his Sunday toupee, finally stepped into the foyer and stared at Darin—and his earring.

"I warned you we might drop in for a surprise visit," her mother said. "We didn't see you at church today."

"I was teaching, Mother. You know I teach on the second and third Sundays of the month."

"Emily, may I see you in the kitchen a moment?" Her mother stalked into the kitchen, and her long nervous fingers began fiddling with the coffee pot.

Emily ground some coffee beans, the whirring sound drowning out her mother's admonitions. When she finished, she poured the grounds into the coffee pot.

"Mom, before you say anything else, I like Darin. Please don't ruin this."

"I don't understand what you mean. Maybe this is your own guilt for having a man in your apartment. On a Sunday no less. Besides, is there something to ruin? I thought you weren't seeing anyone."

"Mom, he's my friend. I've known him a week, and we're not getting married at this point. Okay?"

"I heard he lives in the ghetto."

"As a lay minister, Mom."

"And that he's a gardener."

"A landscape artist, I told you so myself," Emily corrected. "He designs gardens."

"And a garbage man beautifies the neighborhood too. Emily, you're a teacher. How do you expect to raise a family on a gardener's salary?"

"I guess the same way Jesus expected to find His food in the desert. I'm going to trust God that if Darin is the man for me, He will provide."

Silence. Ah, that beautiful sound when her mother was stopped cold in her harsh words.

Something about her not even giving Darin a chance infuriated Emily. She could feel the flame in her cheeks. Emily clenched her teeth to speak.

"Mom, Darin is a godly man. Please don't ruin this for me."

"You keep saying that. What am I ruining if there's nothing going on between you?"

"When you dated Dad, were you willing to announce your engagement in the first week? Or did you want to get to know him a bit before that?"

Her mother's mouth pursed. "I don't remember. I do know, however, that my parents approved."

"I am thirty-two years old! I'm old enough to approve my own boyfriends."

"I just heard from Lois that he brings all these hoodlums to church. That he wears an earring. And I see he doesn't respect his hair, just as I thought."

Emily felt the first prick of tears. Is this what she would become? It was how she treated Grace when Mike first brought her to church, like a throwaway person because she didn't act right, look right.

"Kyle didn't look right either, Mom, and I never met someone who loved the Lord like my brother."

"Your brother couldn't play by the rules!" Nancy Jensen sniffed.

"Whose rules?"

The question hung between them as Darin entered the room. He smiled at her mother, and his natural charm forced a smile to Emily's face.

"Mrs. Jensen, it is so nice to meet you. You have raised a fabulous daughter. My compliments." Darin helped fill the creamer with milk. He'd obviously seen Emily's hands trembling, and when he was finished he stilled her tremor by holding her hands.

"Where did you grow up, young man?"

"Right here in town."

"I heard you're a friend of Fireman Mike's." The small creases at her mother's eyes deepened. She was like a hawk looking for prey.

Emily felt her heart pound against her chest wall. Would Darin explain how he met Mike? Would her mother chase him away too?

thirteen

Darin eyed Mrs. Jensen curiously. She was a strange woman, nothing like her daughter. Where Emily embraced fears and doubts, Mrs. Jensen appeared undaunted and on the offensive. Her eyes were fierce like a wolf's, and she had a spindly frame. To watch mother and daughter side by side, there was no obvious connection, nothing to show a bond or apparent love. Maybe he'd envied Emily's upbringing erroneously.

He cast a glance toward Emily, who was wide-eyed with fear that he would tell his drunk-driving story or, worse yet, his gutter-surviving testimony. She needn't have worried. If Darin had learned anything from his old life, it was when to staple his mouth. Too much information was sometimes the death knell in a conversation, and he had no desire to end this dialogue.

"Yes, I'm a friend of Fireman Mike's." He lifted his voice with enthusiasm. After all, who couldn't love Mike Kingston? "I met him on the job two years ago. And I owe him big thanks because I met your daughter at his wedding." Darin winked at Emily, and her shoulders visibly relaxed.

Mr. Jensen lumbered into the kitchen. Although large in stature, he kowtowed to his wife, but, mostly avoided her. Still, Darin could see that Mr. Jensen had limits.

Emily's dad embraced his daughter, squeezing her with a growl. "We've missed you. You'd hate it there. All it does is

124

rain." He pulled away and looked Darin straight in the eye. "What do you say we all go out to dinner?"

"Only if you let me treat. It isn't every day I get to meet my girlfriend's parents when they live so far away."

"Girlfriend?" Mrs. Jensen tapped her toe against the worn linoleum. "Emily, is this true? I thought you were only friends."

Open mouth, insert foot.

"No, Mother, we're not just friends. He's my boyfriend," Emily said. "To put it in his terms, he's courting me."

Darin stifled a smile at Emily's enjoyment of standing up to her mother. It was obvious that people didn't stand up to Nancy Jensen often. Most likely, it wasn't worth the battle in most instances.

"You're dating a gardener then," she said.

Without thinking, Darin stepped back. There was something both comical and sad about Mrs. Jensen's statement, all at once. Of the many things to disapprove of—his living in the ghetto, his drunk-driving history, even his earring—the vocation surprised him. Granted, he wasn't a Stanford MBA like so many in the Valley, but he made a good living and he had time to enjoy life. The time to mentor troubled youths when most men couldn't break free of their cell phones and constant meetings. As far as he was concerned, he led a pretty good life.

"A gardener who's in love with your daughter," Darin said, almost surprising himself.

Emily shook her head, silently urging him to avoid any confrontation.

Mr. Jensen laughed heartily, his big belly jiggling. "Well, that's the way to tell her. A gardener who's in love with my daughter." He nodded his head in approval. "How do you feel about that, Emily?"

Emily's eyes popped like two light bulbs. "Um. . ."

Mr. Jensen laughed again. "He loves my daughter and he's paying for dinner. Darin is my kind of man." He slapped Darin on the back.

Nancy Jensen remained stiff. The wall between mother and daughter stood firm. Darin wished he could take Emily into his arms and rescue her from such fear. Now he knew why she possessed it. Everything she did was under the studied gaze of Mrs. Jensen.

"Let's go, then," he said loudly. "Mr. Jensen, since you're our aficionado, you can choose the restaurant."

"Since you're paying, I think we should do prime rib."

"Dad!" Emily squealed.

"I'm kidding, Darling. Don't worry. I won't break his wallet before you do." Mr. Jensen's white hair highlighted his steely blue eyes. Every time the man opened his mouth, Darin wondered how he had remained so cheery after a lifetime of living with his wife. The woman emanated no joy at all, but she no doubt knew her Bible inside and out. *The modern-day Pharisee,* he thought.

"McDonald's is taking orders, Mr. Jensen. Do you want a Big Mac or a double cheeseburger?" Darin winked.

"Is that all you can afford?" Mrs. Jensen asked.

"Mom! He just told you he makes good money, and he lives in the ghetto, so costs are low."

"What? You think it's comical that you live in the ghetto? I don't understand you, young man. God would want you to be financially prepared before taking a wife."

Darin watched Emily's countenance falter. They hadn't discussed marriage—not even love. After all, they'd only known each other a week, but Darin felt this was how it must have been during WWII, when you found a bride and knew it. People today wasted too much time in his opinion. God had provided clarity.

Darin hadn't wanted to scare her off, of course, but he knew just as sure as he stood there that Emily was his wife-to-be. He knew the moment he laid eyes on her at Mike's wedding.

Mrs. Jensen was still mumbling something when Emily spoke again. "Mom, Darin is offering us dinner, not a lifetime." She winked at him.

He looked into her eyes and knew instinctively what her heart was saying, that she was apologizing for her mother. Emily wasn't coldhearted like some people at their church believed. She was stifled. She longed to break free of the emotions that bound her. Darin could feel it.

"I hate to be the voice of reason here," Mrs. Jensen said. "But we're a family, and I think our dinner should be reserved for family tonight. Mr. Black, should you hope to become family, I would expect you to respect our time. We've been traveling for two days now, and we'd like to have dinner with our daughter."

The linoleum was spinning. Darin would have respected Mrs. Jensen's wishes if he could not see Mr. Jensen and Emily struggling to protest. It was obvious the two of them would rather leave her behind, not him. The thought forced a nervous chuckle. Would he respect his potential mother-in-law or show his masculinity by standing up to her? It felt a no-win situation. He prayed for God to show him the right direction.

"Mom, Darin and I get together now on Sunday evenings, and I didn't know you were coming," Emily said. "Besides, he's paying so I know Dad wants him along."

Mr. Jensen put his arm around Emily. "That's my little girl. Always watching out for her daddy's pocketbook."

The three of them laughed, but Mrs. Jensen remained stoic. Darin's heart plunged at the sight of her. The woman had forfeited her son, what else would she lose in her unhappiness? He vowed then and there to pray for her every day.

Darin hesitated about going to dinner with the family. It was clear Mrs. Jensen didn't want him to attend, but he thought if he gave into the woman now, he'd never be able to stand up to her. He wanted to respect her, but he also needed to protect Emily. That was his priority. She wanted him to come, and that was all that mattered to him at the moment. Chances were he would never win over Mrs. Jensen.

"Are we ready?" Mr. Jensen asked, a bright smile on his face.

"We are. I know a great place."

Emily's face contorted, and he stifled a laugh. "Don't worry, Emily, it's not my breakfast hole in the wall." He leaned over and whispered in her ear, "I can be classy too."

Visible relief washed over her expression, and he delighted in her joy.

The odd foursome made their way out the door with Mrs. Jensen following behind. One thing Darin knew without question: Emily and her father would pay for their betrayal.

"Mrs. Jensen, is there something you feel like eating for dinner? I have a great restaurant in mind, but it's a steak place. Do you like steak?"

She kept her lips pursed, the angry wrinkles showing themselves easily.

"Steak would be great, don't you think, Dad?" Emily said.

"Any man that would buy me a steak is a good man. Earring and all." Mr. Jensen winked at his daughter.

While her expression spoke volumes, Mrs. Jensen remained quiet.

&

Sundance Steakhouse's neon lights lit up the afternoon sky. The bright blue and white western sky matched Darin's mood—joyous and filled with hope. They were seated right away, and Mrs. Jensen plopped down next to Emily, hoping to discourage him.

"What did you do before you retired, Mr. Jensen?" he asked.

"I sold insurance. I loved it, but it's not the same business nowadays. A man would rather buy a big-screen TV and DVD player than see to his family's long-term care. In my day, a man provided for his family."

"I don't own a TV," Darin said. "Nothing worth watching I'm afraid."

"Not even football?"

"I'd rather be out playing. The guys and I can get a pick-up basketball game any day of the week. I want to do that while I'm young enough to enjoy it."

"You should take up golf. You can do that forever."

"I'm afraid golf is out of my price range," Darin laughed,

but Mrs. Jensen coughed. He supposed he couldn't blame the woman. Who wanted a son-in-law who relied upon God to see to financial needs? One who risked losing his job every time he took a morning off to speak on drunk driving. He wished he could express how much he felt God's call to marry Emily. It was odd: There were so many chasms separating them, the least of which was their difference in education and backgrounds, but Darin was willing to fight for her. Mrs. Jensen may have set her jaw against him, but she had no idea the sheer amount of prayer power she was up against.

"I'm still a member of the club here. Let me take you out sometime this week," Mr. Jensen said.

"Mel, I don't think a beginner on the course is exactly what they expect at the country club."

"Who cares what they expect? I've kept up my membership. I can bring anyone I care to. I just want to see if the boy likes the game."

"He just told you he can't afford to play it, so what does it matter?"

"Nancy, stay out of it," Mr. Jensen warned.

"What are you having, Mom?"

"I'm not hungry."

"So a salad, then?"

"Mel, I want to go home." It was a challenge, not a request, and Mr. Jensen squared his shoulders.

"Well, we're having dinner with our daughter." He turned back toward Darin. "So you think you can get a morning off this week?"

"Sure I can," Darin replied happily. "Who knows? Maybe I'm the next Tiger Woods. Mrs. Jensen, do you play?"

Again, rather than answer, Emily's mother just threw him a glance, as though he were a mere buzzing noise.

Emily excused herself to wash her hands, and Mr. Jensen decided to follow her lead. Mrs. Jensen looked like a hawk going in for the kill. She was obviously anxious to speak to him alone, and he shifted in his seat waiting for the onslaught. Sure enough, as soon as father and daughter were out of sight, Mrs. Jensen spoke.

"It's very charming that you find my daughter so attractive. But she's not for you. She's been a good girl her whole life, and she deserves a man who's done the same for himself. I don't mean to be rude, but she's better than the likes of you. Do you understand that?"

"I don't mean to be disrespectful, Mrs. Jensen, but Emily's husband is God's choice. Not yours. I believe I'm that man and hope that someday Emily and you will see things that way as well."

"Over my dead body, you are."

Darin sat back in his chair. That statement made things abundantly clear. *Lord, make me sure of this. Because I feel certain Emily is who you have for my wife, and from the sound of things, it's going to be an uphill battle.*

fourteen

Emily changed the sheets on her bed so her parents could sleep comfortably in her room. She had already made up the sofa for herself. Her mother hovered, leaning against the doorjamb in the bedroom. Emily tried to ignore the piercing eyes and especially avoid the subject of Darin. Everything was happening so fast. He'd said he was in love with her. In love with her! They barely knew one another, and yet she couldn't help but think the feelings were reciprocal.

"You need to tuck the corners," her mother chided.

"Sorry, Mom, I forgot you liked it that way. I don't like to be stuck under the sheets at night. I feel like I'm in a straightjacket." Emily tucked the sheets, making the corners so tight a Marine would be proud.

"You should do it for yourself. Someday a husband won't want to get into a sloppily made bed like that."

"With the right lingerie I imagine he would."

"Emily Jensen, what a foul mouth!"

Emily bit her lip. "I'm sorry, Mother. I was just making a joke."

"Are you sleeping with that man?"

"Absolutely not! Mother, it was a joke. I just don't think most people care about a perfectly made bed like you do. Kyle never did." She stopped breathing. Had she really mentioned her long-lost brother's name? His name had been forbidden for years, but she suddenly felt empowered, and she searched her mother's face for a reaction.

Mrs. Jensen gasped and fell back onto the bed, her hand over her heart. "Where did we go wrong, Emily?"

"Oh, Mother, spare me the dramatics. I've seen that act before. It's amazing you never do it where a sofa or bed isn't there to catch you."

"We've told you not to mention your brother. He was dead to us when he joined that cult."

"He did not join a cult, Mother. He went into the mission field. You're the one who told him not to contact you if he made the choice. You left Kyle no options, and he was just doing what he was supposed to do."

"Kyle disrespected his parents' wishes. The Bible says to honor your mother and father."

"That doesn't mean doing whatever they say as an adult, Mom. Kyle was listening to a call from God. He wanted to share the Word with the people of the South American jungles. The Great Commission, Mother. Leave and cleave and all that."

"We supported plenty of missionaries in our day. There was no reason for a boy with his education and skills to go jaunting off into a third-world country. It's the same with that boy of yours. He could get himself an education and find a nice job, but he'd rather be traipsing about in the ghetto, talking to kids who don't listen to him. Dodging bullets all the while. Not getting a real job. You think I'm cruel, Emily." Her mother got up from the bed and helped finish with the bedspread. "But you mark my words, you were created for better than this. You'll be miserable if you marry that gardener."

Emily lowered herself slowly onto the bed. A revelation of sorts fell upon her. "Mother, are you happy?" The truth was she had never met a more miserable person than her mother. "Are you?"

"Of course I am. I'm very well-respected in the church. When I told Pastor something, he always listened. I have the gift of administration. You'd be wise to listen to me on matters of the heart such as this. It's not just an emotional decision. You must live with the consequences for the rest of your life."

"You never gave Kyle a choice in his consequences." Emily focused on a painting above her bed. "Will you give me one?" The phone rang. "I'm going to get that. Dad's watching the news. He'll be in later. Sleep tight, Mother."

"Tell your father not to keep you up too late. You've got work tomorrow." The phone continued to ring. "Who is calling you so late?"

Emily grabbed the portable phone. "I'm about to find out. Goodnight, Mother." Running from the room, she picked up the phone. "Hello."

"Hi," Darin's smooth baritone answered.

She felt a blush rise into her cheeks. "Hi, yourself." She shut herself in the utility room for some privacy. The blaring television set made it difficult to hear, but when she slid the door shut, quiet prevailed. "Did you survive dinner with my parents?"

"I did, and I plan to invite myself over later in the week too. They're staying until Saturday, you know."

Emily scrunched up her nose. "No, I didn't hear that. Thanks for being the bearer of bad news. Rosencrantz and Gildenstern have a run for their money," she quipped, referring to Hamlet's messengers.

"Am I supposed to understand that? I know the difference between a dahlia and a tulip, you know. That's my area of expertise." Darin laughed. "So, as I was saying, I'm coming over sometime this week."

"You might just have to eat my cooking then."

"Is that a bad thing?"

"Depends on who you ask. It's not a great thing, that's for certain." She giggled. What a strange sound to hear. She couldn't remember the last time she really laughed, and her laughter was genuine, not a flirtatious act of cuteness, but real and heartfelt. "I make a mean pot roast and can boil up an excellent hot dog. If you're looking for a soufflé, you might want to head elsewhere."

"Pot roast and hot dogs? Well, what else does one need? We can throw some cabbage in the water, and voilà, dinner! Better a meal of vegetables with love than a fattened calf with hatred."

"Like tonight's steak dinner with my mother, you mean?'

"Your mother just wants what's best for you, Emily. You do deserve a man who can afford to golf if he wants. Your father was talking to me about the insurance business."

"Don't you dare!" she exclaimed.

Darin chuckled. "Don't worry, I could barely even get car insurance to drive with my history. Selling life insurance seems unwarranted to me at this point. I prefer the only kind of insurance that pays in full in every circumstance: the gospel."

"Promise me one thing."

"What's that?"

"If our relationship goes anywhere, we won't live within one hundred miles of my mother." Emily said it jokingly, but in her heart she meant every word.

"But your dad was just telling me the house next to them is for sale."

"You are not funny." She slid down the wall onto the floor of the utility room and sighed dreamily. "I miss you already."

"Right back atcha, Babe. I have an idea," Darin said.

"What's that?"

"Let's introduce our mothers to one another and see who does a better job of thwarting this relationship faster. Mine or yours."

"I think there's little question in that. Are you really going golfing with my father?"

"Wouldn't miss it."

"This, from the same man who used to bungee jump? You're going to play a sport where the biggest excitement is a sand wedge shot?"

"Hey, I'm looking forward to wearing some plaid pants and white shoes. Jack Nicklaus is my hero."

"Tiger Woods wears Nike now. Why are you doing this?"

"Because I've met this incredible woman, and I will do whatever I have to. I want her father to know that I will care for his daughter, and my history is just that—my history."

"I don't think it's my father you have to convince. I think it's our mothers."

"So you agree that there's something more here than just friendship."

Emily paused. "I do."

"Now those are words I'm longing to hear. I know I'm coming on fast and furious. I don't mean to scare you, but—"

"Are you still planning to live in East Palo Alto? The former murder capital of the United States?"

"Now come on, that's not fair. EPA has a very small population, and it was a per capita figure. It's not a murder capital anymore."

"That makes all the difference in the world to me, Darin."

"Emily, dive in. The water's great. There are so many real dangers. Why worry about the fake ones?"

Her heart fluttered. How she wanted to dive in, to just seize what she most desired. What she most desired was an outlandish missionary she'd met a mere week ago. But loving him meant giving up all the security she'd known. And suffering her mother's wrath, not to mention his mother's. Was she strong enough to take the risk?

"Real and imagined dangers are a matter of perception."

"Need I remind you my head still throbs from being in your lovely Los Altos neighborhood?"

"Touché."

"There you go speaking in a different language again. Gardener," Darin said. "Please speak slowly. And in English."

"You think you are so funny, Darin Black. Did you not get into Cal Poly's five-year architecture program?"

"Long enough to drop out. Yes, Ma'am, that was me."

"But you know who Rosencrantz is. You did not pass Advanced English in high school without Shakespeare."

"I know who he is," Darin admitted. "But would you like me if I didn't?"

"Maybe even more so," Emily said. "So how's Tuesday night for dinner here?"

"Perfect. You're sure you don't want me to ask my parents?"

"Quite sure. One mother is enough for any dinner party."

"On a more serious note, would you pray for Angel? I'm going to have Pastor call her, and I've vowed to stay away, but don't write her off yet. God is speaking to her."

"Like God spoke to Grace? And my then-boyfriend married her? Like that?"

"Absolutely nothing like that. Just pray she finds God before she finds her next boyfriend. It's like a fix to her, having someone hanging on her arm."

Emily shifted uncomfortably. She wanted to have mercy on Angel, but hearing Darin talk so lovingly about the woman instilled a small seed of fear in her. She'd been in this position before. And it felt too close for comfort.

"See you Tuesday."

"Uh-huh," Emily answered absently. "See you then." Against her better judgment, she prayed with fervor for Angel.

fifteen

Darin splashed water on his face. Lonnie and some of the kids were over watching television, and the constant noise of the wrestling match was beginning to grate on him. It was after 11:00 P.M. and he yawned with exhaustion. With the fire last week at Lonnie's grandma's house, and his own head injury, his calendar had been filled up with emergencies. His laundry stood piled high in the closet, and roommates Pete and Travis worked overtime to unpack Darin's belongings while he selfishly went out to dinner with Emily's parents.

Moving to East Palo Alto became a full-time job in itself. The kids longed for stability and often hung out in the home all hours of the evening. Pete and Travis set hours, but enforcing them often fell to Darin, who was the only one awake late at night. Apparently, his roommates had learned to sleep through everything. Darin dried off his face and headed into the small living room with its secondhand furniture donated by the church.

"Hey, guys, it's time for us to hit the hay. I'm turning into a pumpkin now. Your grandmother's light is still on, Sean," Darin said while looking out the window.

"Dawg, you need to live a little. Going to bed at eleven like my toddler cousin," Lonnie joked.

The three boys laughed, and Darin joined in their friendly banter.

"Dawg, you need to turn in that homework you did tonight, and your slothful self isn't going to want to leave your bed in the morning. Bedtime is being responsible, lounging until ten A.M., pathetic. Unless you're planning to work in a nightclub for a living."

"Hmmm," Sean said, as though thinking about it.

Darin and his roommates had two rules in their ministry home. It was open nearly every night of the week, but closed, unless there was an emergency, at 11:00 P.M. And there was no entrance until homework was produced and finished. Most of the boys had become "A" students just by doing the work given to them at school. Success bred success, because now it had become a way of life thanks to Pete and Travis's rules.

"You just want to get to bed early because you have a girlfriend," Sean said. The boys whistled. "Man, you ain't never gonna get married."

"I'm not?" Darin crossed his arms, anxious to hear their reasoning.

"Nah. What woman is gonna live in this dump?" The three boys broke into laughter.

"Hey!" Darin said. "This is a nice place. And Emily and I can get our own place. Do you really think my wife is going to want roommates, and kids who eat her out of house and home?"

The boys laughed while crunching on a bag of chips.

"The schoolteacher is coming to the hood!" Lonnie clapped his hands in laughter.

Darin wiggled his eyebrows. "Maybe she is coming, and maybe she's given to tutoring slang English until midnight."

"Dude, we're outta here. We're outta here," Lonnie said. He gave Darin a high-five and left. Darin watched the threesome until they entered the home next door. Then he peeked out again, just to make sure they stayed there. At that moment, he collapsed onto the couch and praised God. His life echoed rejoicing in every corner now. He loved gardening and being in the sun all day. He loved coming home to the boys and pick-up basketball, and he loved that Miss Emily Jensen had seen fit to date him. It were as though he were floating above everything that might harm him now. His mother, Emily's mother, their protests meant nothing to him now. God would work it out, Darin had no doubts. She was the woman for him.

Someone knocked at the door, and Darin checked the clock on the wall. It read 11:15. Looking out the peephole, he saw Angel standing there. He quickly opened the door.

"Angel, what on earth are you doing out at this time of night?" He pulled her in. This was the time of night people shot off guns for fun. It was no time to be out alone in a strange city.

Her eyes were red and puffy, and she wore no makeup. "I'm pregnant."

The words hit him with the force of a train. Bile rose in Darin's throat. "Come sit down, Angel." He led her to the sofa and helped her into her seat. This wasn't an act; she trembled, and her expression held true anxiety.

"Does the father know yet?"

She looked away. "He's a professional football player. He's going to think I set him up. He'll give me some money and want me to go away."

Darin paused for a moment. "Did you set him up?"

"No! I should have known you'd ask that. You preaching—"

"Look, I'm not trying to be cruel, but it's a fair question. You haven't mentioned any boyfriend and you show up on my doorstep pregnant."

"It doesn't matter whose it is because I'm getting rid of it."

"It? You're calling your unborn child it? Angel, that's not like you. You always wanted to be a mother."

"Not now I don't. What am I supposed to do, settle down with a baby and give up my cheerleading career? Just because I didn't make the Raiderettes doesn't mean I won't get there next year, or even with the Sabercats in San Jose."

Darin's stomach lurched. Surely, no woman was bad enough to sacrifice a child for a job in cheerleading. He just couldn't believe it, and he didn't know how long he stood there with his mouth hanging open. He'd known Angel a long time. He'd seen countless scenarios where her selfishness surprised him. But even this was beneath her. This was something he wouldn't have expected.

"Angel, please. Promise me you won't do anything rash. This is something that's going to take a lot of thought and prayer."

She rose from her seat and sat in his lap. "This is why I came here," she purred.

Darin tried to wiggle free. He was really worried about Angel now.

"There is one condition under which I will keep this baby."

"What?" he asked, his heart hammering in his chest.

"Marry me, and we raise it as our own."

He pushed her off his legs. "I think you should leave."

"That's just what I thought. You're not willing to put your money where your mouth is on this God thing. You're the same hypocrite you always were."

"Me? Why on earth would you want to marry me if you think I'm such bad news, Angel? You come over here, attack me, tell me you'll kill a child if I won't marry you, then tell me I'm not worthy of being a husband. I don't get it."

"This is hard for me to say, but deep down I think you're the only man for me. I know if you'd search your heart, you'd think that too. Yes, we have our issues, any couple does, but you would care for another man's baby as if it were your own. You know me, Darin. I can't do this alone, and that schoolmarm won't ever make you happy."

"Is everything all right?" Pete stuck his head out his bedroom door.

"Everything's fine," Angel snapped.

Seeing her and knowing her history with Darin, Pete didn't disappear into his room again. He went into the kitchen and noisily started to make a sandwich.

Angel exhaled a tornado-worthy sigh. "I can see we're going to be chaperoned. So I'll just leave you with this decision. How far are you willing to go for this so-called faith of yours, Darin?"

"This doesn't make any sense to me, Angel. Why would you want to marry someone who didn't want to marry you?"

"I don't want to marry someone who doesn't want to marry me. I just don't believe that's true. You loved me once, and even with all this goody-goody business going on in your heart, you will love me again." She stood and tried to kiss him on the lips. He dodged the motion and accepted her kiss on the cheek. "I'll be in touch."

"This is blackmail," he said.

"Your mother and I know the true you resides in there somewhere, Darin. We'll get him back. If it's the last thing we do."

Darin watched her safely to her car and came back into the house where Pete was waiting. Pete's lanky frame bent over a huge submarine sandwich he'd just created. "You want half?" he asked.

"Sure."

They sat together at the table.

"I didn't just hear what I thought I heard," Pete said.

"Angel's pregnant with some football player's baby. She wants to marry me to keep the child."

"Are you sure she's really pregnant?"

"How could I be? She's troubled, Pete. Deeply troubled. She thinks I can solve all her problems, but I can't begin to solve her problems. But if there is a baby, how could I live with myself if I knew I could stop her from. . ." He didn't want to think about it. Nor could he bring himself to say the word.

"When God calls you to ministry full-time, things happen," Pete said. "When I first came here to live, my fiancé wouldn't come with me. She loved the Lord, but she said she just wasn't called here, so I must not be the man for her. That day broke my heart, Darin, but I couldn't break God's. He wanted me here."

"I'm sorry."

"Following God always has a cost. Sometimes it feels too high, but it never is."

"I'm commanded not to marry an unbeliever, but if it costs

life—" Darin shook his head. "God doesn't give that one away in the Bible."

"Hosea married the prostitute."

"You're a big help, Pete, thanks a lot."

"It will cost you either way. Did you think about Emily in all this?"

"I haven't thought about anything. It's just too fresh, too unbelievable. I wonder if my mother knows anything about this."

"Wouldn't surprise me if Angel told your mother it was your baby," Pete said with his mouth full of sandwich.

Darin let his head fall to the table. "I hadn't thought of that," he mumbled. "I was planning to buy an engagement ring soon for Emily. I thought my life was finally falling into place, that I finally understood."

Pete stopped chewing. "You can't marry Angel, Darin. This is a temptation, and I don't believe temptation is sent by God. He can handle it. We just have to pray. In the meantime, you need to let Emily know what's going on. Before she finds out from someone else. Namely Angel or your mother."

Darin downed the last of his sandwich. "Because that's just what Emily needs. Another reason to dump me." He got up to get a glass of milk.

Pete stood to his feet. "Angel knows you're working with the boys on responsible parenting, trying to keep them out of adult situations. She'll use this against you, Darin. You need to come clean right away and let people know this isn't your baby. A life of ministry is always rough to begin with. I think it's a testing period."

Darin slammed a hand on the table. "She's not going to win."

"Don't think of it as her, think of it as the enemy. And God is much more powerful."

Darin skulked to his bedroom. In two years of being a Christian, he'd never felt this low. *Lord, help me. I don't know where to turn.*

sixteen

Emily's mother prepared a gigantic breakfast before work, but the thought of food in the morning nauseated Emily. She'd never been a morning person, preferring food at the 10 A.M. hour, not 6 when she woke up. That time was reserved for coffee. She ate as much as she could stomach before making excuses to leave. She'd stop at the coffee shop on her way to school and purchase a tall latte.

At three dollars a pop, such java luxuries weren't everyday occurrences on her teacher's salary, but today, with her mother's constant nagging about Darin, it felt like an investment worth making for the mere escape. If she had any doubts about Darin and her future, her mother's incessant complaints against him made her feelings even stronger. Hearing her mother's fears expressed only made Emily realize that she loved Darin, despite the obvious differences between them.

For example, he was a gardener. There was such a purity about the fact that Darin worked with his hands, that he'd given up chasing the corporate dream like so many of the fathers she knew. Some of these men had forfeited their families for the opportunity to be a corporate vice president while Darin made the kids of EPA his priority. Kids he hadn't even fathered. Her mother kept rehashing that Darin couldn't afford to play the game of golf. Well, then Darin also couldn't afford to spend every Saturday away from his family like her own father had always done. Emily hoped she'd be the kind of wife that Darin didn't want to avoid. Bitter memories boiled up. Did her father avoid their home, and thus her mother? She prayed she would never be that kind of wife.

"Bye, Dad, I'll see you this afternoon. Mom, thanks for the breakfast. It was terrific."

"You didn't eat a thing, Emily. Don't you teach your kids at school about a healthy breakfast? It's the most important meal of the day they say."

"Sure I teach them. I just don't practice what I preach in that case." She giggled. "If I eat in the morning, I'm hungry all day." *But a latte, now that's a different matter altogether.*

"Leave her alone, Nancy. She's not a child," her dad said. "We're going to the beach today, Emily. Do you want to meet us over there for dinner? We can eat at the Chart House, your favorite."

"Oh, Dad, I'd love to, but I really need to catch up on lesson plans. I've been so social this weekend. I haven't finished my plans for the week. You know how it bothers me to be unprepared."

Her mother clanked a dish into the sink. "You certainly have been a bit too social. Don't give up your job for a man who might not be around in two weeks. I would think your short-lived relationship with that fireman would have taught you something."

"Mom, I was talking about you and Dad coming to

California by surprise. I generally work on my stuff Sunday afternoons. While I love having you, it did throw a kink into my schedule."

"Hmmph." Her mother pursed her lips.

The phone rang, much to Emily's relief. She raced to get it before her mother answered and gave someone the third degree. Her phone rarely rang in the morning, and she couldn't help but throw up a prayer before answering.

"Hello."

"Emily, it's Darin."

"Darin, is everything okay? You don't sound so good."

"It's nothing for you to worry about, but I just called Pastor Fredericks's office and got an appointment with him today at four. It's usually his day off, but he's making an exception for me. Do you think you could meet me there? I want to tell both of you at the same time."

"Tell us what?" Emily's heart hammered against her chest. Was this where he told her he was already married? Or where he explained his life of crime back in Brazil or something?

"Emily, please trust me, and wait on this one. I can tell you it's not as bad as you're thinking."

"But you want me to meet you at the church? What's this about?"

"It's something I can't talk about on the phone, but I'd really love for you to be there. It concerns you in an off-hand way. It concerns our future." The seriousness in his voice alarmed her. She wasn't used to Darin being evasive with answers. Was there more to his ministry that she didn't understand? More than she would be able to handle?

"I'll meet you there at four o'clock." Emily decided she just had to trust God for the day. But within her heart she prayed there was nothing more. Nothing she couldn't handle. She had quickly fallen in love with Darin. Would her heart be dashed as it had been so many times before? Would Darin leave like Kyle had? Like Fireman Mike had? She felt sick. A whole day of not knowing, just waiting for the other shoe to fall.

Emily offered her mother's questioning glances no satisfaction. "I'll see you both tonight. I take it I'm not cooking for you then, you're eating out?"

"Do you really think we should waste the money, Dear? I can get something for us all at the grocery today." Her mother grabbed her purse, as if ready to go.

"We'll eat over on the coast tonight, Nancy. That way Emily won't feel in any hurry to get home and entertain us. It sounds like she has enough going on today." Her father turned toward her. "We'll be home by about eight. That will give you time to get caught up on lessons."

"Before they fire you from that job," her mother added.

"Tenure, Mom. It's a beautiful thing."

After a peaceful latte and a morning newspaper at her local coffeehouse, Emily rushed into her classroom to find her principal waiting. She looked at the clock nervously, but she was on time. "Mr. Walker, is everything all right? What can I do for you?"

She hoped he hadn't noticed her absentmindedness lately. A mere two weeks ago, Emily had no social life, and her work could never be questioned, but lately she lived in her own little world. Going to the city on a weeknight, staying all hours at the local hospital, and filling out police reports. Dating Darin was certainly not for the faint of heart.

Mr. Walker cleared his throat and looked toward the white board with the morning's assignment written on it. Emily silently thanked God she'd been prepared on Friday. "Miss Jensen, one of your students was in an accident over the weekend."

Her throat caught and words tumbled from her mouth. "An accident? Who was it? May the Lord have watched over them!"

"I understand your religious beliefs, Miss Jensen, and of course I tolerate your first-amendment rights, but I'll need to make sure this kind of speech doesn't come from you when you tell the rest of the class."

"Is someone hurt?" Emily asked, ignoring the admonition. One of her children's fate lay in the balance, and Mr. Walker could only worry about the liberal lawyers in California waiting to pounce.

"Not seriously. David Bronson's car was hit by a drunk driver this weekend. His whole family is fine, but David is in the hospital with a broken collarbone. You might want to have the class make him a card or an art project. I told his mother you would visit this afternoon and bring any homework."

Homework. Leave it to Mr. Walker to be concerned about the homework of a first-grader when the boy could have lost his life. Had the school administration lost all sense of decorum? Of rational behavior?

Mr. Walker ignored her shock. "I'm contacting MADD today. Apparently, they have a drunk driver with a history of this kind of criminal background. He's actually reformed and is supposed to be excellent talking with children. He has a way of bringing it home, they say."

"What's his name?" Emily asked tentatively.

"Not sure. It's that Fireman Mike's friend. Remember that trouble-making mother you had last year? That delinquent boy Josh of hers? Well, this is a friend of her husband's. Oh, wait a minute, you used to date that fireman yourself, didn't you?"

"Briefly." *Mr. Tact. Briefly.*

"We'll have an assembly at the end of the week. Hopefully, David will be back to school by then, but if not we can still emphasize the importance of seat belt safety. They said if David hadn't been in his booster seat, he wouldn't be coming back to us."

Emily clutched her heart. Her principal seemed to lack any feeling for children but loved edicts as if Robert's Rules of Order were written upon his heart. She suddenly realized he bore a striking resemblance to her mother. And for a moment, she seethed at the sight of him. With one more word she couldn't trust herself. Rules first. People second. Would her life ever be spared of people who ordered their life so?

David Bronson exuded charm. He was the kind of kid who could get into trouble, smile, say something sweet, and make it all go away instantaneously. All the girls loved David, and he was the first boy Emily had ever seen dominate the first-grade love note competition. One day he'd be a grown-up Darin Black. Charming, confident, and in many ways free of life's consequences. It were as though the two of them, David and Darin, had a dozen angels on full-time watch helping to break any falls.

Mr. Walker broke her reverie. "I'm a little worried about bringing the drunk driver here. He is a felon after all, but I think it will do more good than harm if we keep him chaperoned the entire time."

"I don't think it's something we need to worry about. Who knows? He might even be an upstanding citizen now."

"Phht, just like Charlie Manson is a reformed citizen now."

Emily clenched her teeth. "I'm dating that drunk driver. And do you know what? I might even see fit to marry him, so I'd appreciate it if you'd take your prejudices elsewhere. He's a Christian now, and he's changed." She stood with her mouth open, wondering if she'd really spoken her thoughts aloud. She watched Mr. Walker for an indication, but he said nothing. She scratched her chin, and like a gorilla in the zoo the principal did the same thing.

"I don't know what's gotten into you, Emily, but I am watching you. Closely." His brows furrowed into an angry V. Mr. Walker was antagonistic toward religion of any sort. Well, that wasn't exactly true. If it reeked of tolerance and ethnic background, it was more than accepted. He despised talk of the Bible, however, and he'd tried to force Emily's Bible from her desk on countless occasions. She now kept it in her drawer.

She had no doubt that if Darin's faith was announced at his speech, he'd never be allowed to speak in the schools again. Mr. Walker would see to that.

seventeen

Emily watched the clock tick for what felt like an eternity. *Tick. Tick. Tick.* At 2:28, she practically cried out for the bell to ring. When it finally did, she called "Class dismissed!"

She sighed, quickly planned for the next day's lesson, and headed to the church to meet Darin. Her stomach was in knots at the thought of seeing him. She could picture his face, and her heart did somersaults at the mere thought of his strong jaw.

Darin stood outside the office, a big bouquet of peach roses in his hand. She drew in a deep breath. How she loved that man. She loved that man! Was it even possible? She giggled like a kindergartner. She hadn't felt such joy since her college graduation, a time when she thought the world was fresh and full of promise. It held promise once again, and she closed her eyes. "Thank You, God. Thank You for this man."

When she opened her eyes, Darin stood in front of her, the roses perched under her nose. "They smell divine," she said. "Are they for me?"

"They'll never be for anyone else, but, Emily, things are going to get rough. I need to tell you about the dilemma I'm in, and I want Pastor there to speak truth to me because I'm in love with you. You and no one else. But life is so valuable to me, so precious. And I know you feel the same way about children."

Emily pushed the roses back toward him. "You have a child somewhere?"

He dropped his head, the light red stubble appearing. "I don't have a child, not one that's my own anyway. Promise me something, Emily. You'll hear the whole story before you run out."

She clutched her stomach. Why didn't anything come easily to her? Why did everything have to be strife-filled? "Darin, I don't know if I can handle any more bad news. I haven't told you the whole story of my brother."

"Now's a good time."

"We had a next-door neighbor. A little boy who was badly abused by his mother. We didn't call it that then, we just thought she was mean and spanked him too much." She fiddled with the collar on her shirt. "The little boy disappeared one day. We found out later he'd been taken to the hospital and eventually taken from his mother. My brother rebelled, vowing not to be hurt when my mother disciplined us harshly. But she never hurt us, it was just his reaction. So he left."

"Mike hinted there was something haunting about your history."

"I became a caretaker, baby-sitter for the neighborhood, one-time child psychology major, but I changed it to teacher. It was too hard for me to see how many children were hurt by people who should love them."

Darin shifted his weight, and just by his reaction Emily realized she'd probably said too much. Whatever was on his mind, he didn't need her drumming up past hurts of her own.

"Darin, Emily, you're both here. Good." Pastor Fredericks greeted them each with a handshake and brought them into his office. "I've just been on hospital visits. Come on in and sit down." He waved a hand toward two red chairs before his desk. "Do you mind if I open us with prayer?" He bowed his head and dedicated the time to the Lord.

"Pastor, I have a big problem with an old friend from my past."

"The young woman named Angel?"

"Exactly."

Emily closed her eyes instinctively, as if she might not be able to hear by doing so. She knew Darin didn't love Angel, so what did any of this have to do with her? "Darin, maybe it's better if I wait outside."

"No, Emily," he said with force. "You're here because I love you, and I want you to know the truth. If I tell you in front of Pastor, you'll have no reason to doubt me."

So this was where she was told good-bye. Abandoned for the other woman, the other woman who needed him so much more. She braced herself.

Darin stood and walked the length of the office back and forth. "Pastor, Emily, Angel is pregnant, or so she says. It's not my baby. I swear to you that there's no way it could be my baby. But she's given me an ultimatum. I can either marry her and raise this child as my own, or she will take care of it in her own way."

Emily circled herself with her arms. A child's life hung in the balance. Just like when Josh needed Fireman Mike for a father, this baby would need Darin. She closed her eyes and nodded her head, trying to get her heart to accept the fact that Darin was going away, but for good reason. Kyle had gone away for good reasons too, but she still felt her brother's absence acutely every single day.

"You're not going to like what I have to say, Darin." Pastor Fredericks stood.

"But I'm willing to listen. That's why I'm here."

"The Bible says you are not to marry an unbeliever. You know Angel is an unbeliever, am I right?"

"Yes, Pastor, but—"

"Darin, you have the heart of an evangelist, and just like all spiritual gifts, there's a downside to this gift. It's thinking you can do God's work for Him, if only you try hard enough. I take it you're willing to live a life of sacrifice for a woman who's made some terrible life choices and wants to pull you down with her."

Emily stood up. "I should go. I don't feel that I belong here."

"Sit down, Emily," Pastor Fredericks ordered, and she did so. "You've stepped back enough times and given away things that are rightfully yours. Now I don't know if you and Darin are meant to be married, but I will not have you back away from this because of a woman's schemes. You're both going to listen to me. You asked for my opinion and you are more than going to get it."

Darin grabbed her hand and clenched it tightly. She squeezed back. *I love you,* she thought silently.

"What is it you want to do, Darin?"

"I want to marry Emily."

Her heart swelled. Hearing those words from such a man was more than she ever hoped for. All her years of teaching, all her love for family, nothing matched hearing those words from Darin Black.

"Then why would you go against the Bible, marry a woman you don't love, who may or may not be pregnant, and quit your ministry in East Palo Alto? Because I'm willing to bet this woman is not willing to live in the ghetto. Am I right?"

"You make it sound so simple, Pastor. But is it really? She's carrying a child she's threatening to destroy. Can I live with that my entire life?"

"I don't think you have a choice, Darin. This isn't yours. This is God's to handle. You cannot devote your entire life to the salvation of one person which may or may not happen. And in the meantime, you would hurt the woman you do love and let her live alone? God wants authenticity, Darin. He doesn't want sacrifice to the point of sin. He's already been the sacrifice."

Darin raked through his stubbly hair, and relief flooded his face. He lowered himself onto the burgundy carpet and perched himself on one knee in front of Emily. She wanted to touch the soft red stubble on his head, and this time she didn't stop her hand.

"Emily Jensen, I love you. I've got issues, you can hear that as plain as the organ in church. Your mother hates me, I'm going to be poor as long as I can imagine, but I love you with my whole heart. I prayed like you can't believe that Pastor would tell me I owed Angel nothing. I don't love her. I never did, and I had such guilt over her bad choices. I wanted to fix her, like Jesus did for me."

"I understand." And she did.

"What I'm trying to do, very badly I must say, is ask you to be my wife. Emily, will you marry me?"

Tears of joy sprang forth, and Emily lowered herself onto the carpet and sobbed into his shoulder. "Yes, yes, I will marry you."

Pastor Fredericks coughed. "Now I think it's me that should leave." He stepped through the door and closed it behind him.

"Do you think if we offered to care for Angel's baby she might carry it?"

Darin's smile faded. "Emily, you would do that?"

"I told you, I've spent my entire life caring for other people's children. I thought I'd never have any of my own. Raising a child with you is what I want. Where it comes from is the least of my concerns."

"Praise God for you, Emily. Praise God. He has blessed me so."

Emily clutched her heart. "I'm still having trouble breathing. A minute ago, I thought you were marrying another woman. Now—"

"Now I'm doing what I'm truly called to do, not feeling guilty about something that only God can fix."

"We'll pray for Angel every day, Darin."

"We will," he agreed.

A quiet knock invaded their privacy. Pastor Fredericks poked his head in the door. "Are you two done with my office?" He winked.

Emily felt the heat rise into her face. "Thank you, Pastor, we are."

"Emily and I are engaged."

"Have you told her parents?"

A little bit of Emily's joy died within. "No, but we're on our way."

"First, we'd like to pray with you, Pastor. It seems the world is stacked against us, and yet I've never felt so within God's will. Not since I moved to East Palo Alto."

"East Palo Alto," Emily mumbled. "I'm going to live in East Palo Alto."

The corner of Darin's mouth turned up, and he reached his hand to her jaw. "You're going to live with me."

She exhaled. "I'm going to live with my husband." A few weeks ago, she thought she'd never get married. Now the man of her dreams was standing before her, professing his love. In front of their pastor no less. If only her mother would understand, everything would be perfect.

eighteen

Nothing is ever perfect, Emily lamented. She paced her apartment. Her parents would understand, they just had to. She looked at the clock and watched the second-hand click away the minutes until Darin arrived. She knew she must tell her parents before he did, but every time she clutched the doorknob, the sick feeling in her stomach began. She squared her shoulders and reached one more time, this time opening the door.

"Dad," she yelled over the television set. "Can you turn that off for a moment? I have something to tell you both."

Her mother looked up at her from over her magazine. "This had better not be about that hoodlum."

"It is about Darin," Emily said. *I will not live in fear.*

"Surely, you're not thinking of anything serious with him."

"Nancy, be quiet and let your daughter speak," her dad said. "She's a grown woman."

"Mom, Dad, Darin and I are getting married. I'm going to live in East Palo Alto, but I'll still teach for the time being in Los Altos."

Nancy Jensen gasped and swooned as if she might pass out.

"I know this comes as a surprise to you both, but I just know this is God's plan for my life. I don't think it will be easy, or even romantic at times, but I'm following His lead, and Darin's as well."

"I forbid it," her mother said. "I absolutely forbid you to throw your life away on a gardener who lives in the ghetto. He wears an earring, Emily. We raised you better than that."

Mel Jensen stood and placed his fists on his hips. "That's enough, Nancy. You will rejoice in your daughter's joy regardless of your opinions. I lost my son because of your constant nagging. I won't lose my daughter too." His words came like daggers. The memories of the terrible battle before her brother left still haunted her. She couldn't let her own marriage break apart her parents.

"Please don't fight. There's nothing to fight about. This isn't your decision. It's mine. Mom, I understand this is not the way you would have it. But I'm happy, and he's a strong Christian. He's just not the Christian we expected."

"I suppose you expect me to pay for this—oh, I can't even call it a wedding." She crossed her arms and practically spit her words.

"Nancy, I'm warning you."

"If you support her in this harebrained idea, I will leave right now."

Emily's father planted his feet on the carpet. "Do what you have to do."

"No, no. Please don't do this!" Emily cried.

"Emily, if you back down on this, she will rule our lives forever. Is that what you want? Do you think her version of Christianity is what you want to live for the rest of your life? Because I've lived it for far too long, and I can testify it's like selling your very soul to please her. Do you want to please your mother or God?"

She choked back her emotion. "I want to please both."

"And if that isn't possible?" he asked.

Emily stared at her mother's hard expression. She would end up as Kyle had, coming from nowhere, her family legacy lost in one life choice. A choice for a man she barely knew. Yet she felt God calling her toward him as clearly as if He'd whispered the word Darin in her ear.

"I don't know," she admitted. She searched her mother's eyes. Eyes that wouldn't meet her own. "Please, Mother, look at me."

A look of disgust crossed her mother's expression. "You're not the daughter I raised."

"Yes, I am the daughter you raised, Mother. You just don't like it because I'm different from you, but God made me this way. I am His creation. Darin is His creation. We are in His image, not yours." She couldn't believe all that was tumbling from her mouth. She knew it might cost her a relationship with her mother. Something she swore she'd never let happen. But her father's encouragement spurred her onward. "Do you think that all Christians must look as you do?"

A knock at the door left the three of them looking at one another, each wondering who was going to open the door. Minutes passed, and finally the door opened on its own. Darin stood framed in the doorway.

"Is everything okay?" he asked.

"No. My mother will not be attending our wedding. Apparently, she is not happy about our news." Bitterness dripped from Emily's words.

Darin looked at the floor, then at Nancy Jensen. "I'm sorry

to hear that. Your daughter will be a beautiful bride. We'll miss you."

Emily loved his firmness, yet her insides squirmed. She wanted it all. She wanted a husband and her family.

"Your father will be there to walk you down the aisle, Emily," her dad said.

"Thank you, Dad," she said huskily.

"This is the way it's going to be then?"

"It doesn't have to be, Mrs. Jensen." Darin walked away from Emily, looking her mother in the eyes. His expression gentle, he took her hand. "I'll spend my life proving I was right for your daughter. Whether or not you choose to watch is your decision, but I will miss you greatly in our life. I will miss you as a grandmother to our future children, and, most importantly, a mother to your wonderful daughter."

For the first time Emily could ever remember, she saw her mother's eyes fill with tears. Real tears. Not the kind that she often used with Emily's father for manipulation, but real tears.

"I don't ever want to hear about your mistake," she said to Emily.

"You won't."

"And you'd better keep my daughter safe in the ghetto or I'll come after you personally."

"Yes, Ma'am!" Darin saluted. "My parents are waiting in the car outside. Are you ready, Emily?"

"Ready as I'm going to be."

Darin went outside, and when he appeared again, his mother was with him, her black mascara running down her cheeks. His father came in behind her, looking at the television, most likely upset at missing some sports event. Emily headed toward him.

"Hi, Mr. Black. Mrs. Black, nice to see you under better circumstances."

"Let's just get this over with," Mrs. Black said. "You're marrying my son. None of us has any choice, so when's the date?"

Emily looked at Darin, who slapped his forehead. "Mom!"

"I think that guy hit you over the head harder than you're aware of," Mrs. Black snapped. "I'm hoping this wedding will at least be after the trial. It's not going to look good to have your wife testify against this guy."

"There is no trial, Mom. He was wanted on other charges, so he's just in jail for that now. If there is, I think her testimony is quite clear on the police report."

"You both plan to go through with this? You are aware my son is not a college graduate?" she asked Emily.

Emily nodded.

"And that he goes through phases which don't last very long. I'll admit this Jesus-thing has lasted awhile, but when he wants to race cars and parasail, where will you be?"

"I guess I'll be at his side." Emily's stomach felt like she'd just jumped from a cliff. Where would following Darin lead? It didn't matter.

Darin spoke up. "We know how you all feel about this wedding, and we're sorry you're not happier for us. It's happened fast. We still have so much to learn about each other, but I'm following my gut here. I love this woman. I can't explain how it happened so quickly, I only know it will never happen like this again. When I had my accident, I learned to grasp life for all it's worth."

Emily watched her mother wince, and she took a step

closer to Darin, fitting her hand into his. Her heart pounded at the four worried expressions facing them. She'd never done anything like this, never dared to go against anyone else's wishes, but looking into Darin's green eyes, she couldn't defy what she felt in her heart.

"We'd like to take you all to dinner," Darin said. "I don't expect you to fall in love with the idea, but I hope you'll get more comfortable with our decision, and get to know one another."

Emily's mother shook her head. "I'm not going to get comfortable with the decision because it's not going to happen."

Mel Jensen clenched his teeth. "It is going to happen all right. Get over it, or I'm done."

"What?"

"You heard me," he whispered. "I don't want to make a scene, but I'm not sitting for this. Mrs. Black, this goes for you as well. No one is going to ruin my baby girl's happiness. She loves this man, and that's good enough for me."

Guilt welled up in Emily's chest. She felt so torn by the conflict all around her. But then she embraced the most comforting thought. Kyle would want her to stand up for her rights. This was not just for Darin and herself. This choice was for Kyle.

"Thank you, Daddy." She kissed him on the cheek then kissed her mother. The elder woman went stone cold, her face rigid with anger. Emily squeezed Darin's hand for strength.

epilogue

two years later

Grandma Jensen put the baby boy down in his crib and offered a light kiss. "You are the most beautiful baby ever born. God shined His grace upon you, little one."

Emily nearly cried at the sight of her mother bent over the bassinet. Who would have imagined that such hard women as her mother and mother-in-law would melt at the warmth of a single, precious baby boy. She looked up when she heard Emily.

"I hope you and Darin will consider moving up by us, Emily. It's not fair for you to keep our grandchild from us. And to raise him in this neighborhood. It's unthinkable."

Emily laughed. "Are you kidding? With all the free baby-sitting I get in this neighborhood with Darin's Bible study kids? I'm not going anywhere. Besides, Grandma Black would wrestle you to the floor if you took her favorite little man."

Darin walked into the tiny house, and Emily met him in the hallway. "Hi, Love. How was another day in paradise?" he asked.

"Perfect, as usual. Andrew started to roll over today. It won't be long now."

Darin sighed. "Did you get it on videotape?"

"Of course."

"It's a wonder anything in that child's life will ever happen without being caught on video," Grandma Jensen said. "Poor little thing. He needs his grandma just so his mother can carry the camera."

Darin laughed out loud. "He does need his grandma. You know, Mom, the house up the street is for sale."

Emily giggled. "Right, Darin. My mother is going to move to the ghetto, as she calls it."

Nancy Jensen pursed her lips. "I'll move anywhere for my grandchild, Emily. Don't be smart."

The doorbell broke their conversation, which Emily could only hope was a joke. She opened the door to see the most handsome face she'd ever seen besides her husband's. She couldn't breathe and had to find a chair when oxygen failed to creep into her nose.

"Can I help you?" Darin said threateningly.

"I heard I was an uncle."

Emily buried her face in her hands and soon felt her brother's arms wrap around her. "Is it really you?"

"I've been in South America. I got word from my supporters that my sister had a baby. I couldn't take a chance he'd grow up uncool. So I came to teach him."

She clutched her brother in her arms and held on for as long as he'd let her. When Kyle pulled away she noticed he'd grown a beard, but other than that and a few wrinkles around the eyes, he was the same brother she'd last seen ten years before.

She looked to her mother, who blinked steadily to force her tears away. Then Nancy Jensen ran to the son who had left so long ago. "I'm sorry, Kyle. I'm so very sorry," she sobbed.

Emily looked into her husband's eyes. "I will become even more undignified than this," she said, quoting Darin's life Scripture. And she would. Because fear had rendered her useless, but jumping off of life's precipice provided her with daily, unending joy.

A Letter To Our Readers

Dear Reader:

In order that we might better contribute to your reading enjoyment, we would appreciate your taking a few minutes to respond to the following questions. We welcome your comments and read each form and letter we receive. When completed, please return to the following:

Fiction Editor
Heartsong Presents
PO Box 719
Uhrichsville, Ohio 44683

Did you enjoy reading *An Unbreakable Hope* by Kristin Billerbeck?

❏ Very much! I would like to see more books by this author!
❏ Moderately. I would have enjoyed it more if

_____
_____
_____

Are you a member of **Heartsong Presents**? ❏ Yes ❏ No
If no, where did you purchase this book? _____
_____

How would you rate, on a scale from 1 (poor) to 5 (superior), the cover design? _____

On a scale from 1 (poor) to 10 (superior), please rate the following elements.

____ Heroine	____ Plot
____ Hero	____ Inspirational theme
____ Setting	____ Secondary characters

5. These characters were special because?_____

_____

_____

6. How has this book inspired your life?_____

_____

_____

7. What settings would you like to see covered in future
   Heartsong Presents books? _____

_____

_____

8. What are some inspirational themes you would like to see
   treated in future books? _____

_____

_____

9. Would you be interested in reading other **Heartsong
   Presents** titles?   ❏ Yes   ❏ No

10. Please check your age range:
    ❏ Under 18   ❏ 18-24
    ❏ 25-34   ❏ 35-45
    ❏ 46-55   ❏ Over 55

Name_____

Occupation _____

Address _____

City_____ State_____ Zip_____

Heart♥ong

Any 12
Heartsong
Presents titles
for only
$30.00*

CONTEMPORARY ROMANCE IS CHEAPER BY THE DOZEN!

Buy any assortment of twelve *Heartsong Presents* titles and save 25% off of the already discounted price of $3.25 each!

*plus $2.00 shipping and handling per order and sales tax where applicable.

HEARTSONG PRESENTS TITLES AVAILABLE NOW:

__HP197 *Eagle Pilot*, J. Stengl
__HP205 *A Question of Balance*, V. B. Jones
__HP206 *Politically Correct*, K. Cornelius
__HP210 *The Fruit of Her Hands*, J. Orcutt
__HP213 *Picture of Love*, T. H. Murray
__HP217 *Odyssey of Love*, M. Panagiotopoulos
__HP218 *Hawaiian Heartbeat*, Y.Lehman
__HP221 *Thief of My Heart*, C. Bach
__HP222 *Finally, Love*, J. Stengl
__HP225 *A Rose Is a Rose*, R. R. Jones
__HP226 *Wings of the Dawn*, T. Peterson
__HP234 *Glowing Embers*, C. L. Reece
__HP242 *Far Above Rubies*, B. Melby & C. Wienke
__HP245 *Crossroads*, T. and J. Peterson
__HP246 *Brianna's Pardon*, G. Clover
__HP261 *Race of Love*, M. Panagiotopoulos
__HP262 *Heaven's Child*, G. Fields
__HP265 *Hearth of Fire*, C. L. Reece
__HP278 *Elizabeth's Choice*, L. Lyle
__HP298 *A Sense of Belonging*, T. Fowler
__HP302 *Seasons*, G. G. Martin
__HP305 *Call of the Mountain*, Y. Lehman
__HP306 *Piano Lessons*, G. Sattler
__HP317 *Love Remembered*, A. Bell
__HP318 *Born for This Love*, B. Bancroft
__HP321 *Fortress of Love*, M. Panagiotopoulos
__HP322 *Country Charm*, D. Mills
__HP325 *Gone Camping*, G. Sattler
__HP326 *A Tender Melody*, B. L. Etchison
__HP329 *Meet My Sister, Tess*, K. Billerbeck
__HP330 *Dreaming of Castles*, G. G. Martin
__HP337 *Ozark Sunrise*, H. Alexander
__HP338 *Somewhere a Rainbow*, Y. Lehman
__HP341 *It Only Takes a Spark*, P. K. Tracy
__HP342 *The Haven of Rest*, A. Boeshaar

__HP349 *Wild Tiger Wind*, G. Buck
__HP350 *Race for the Roses*, L. Snelling
__HP353 *Ice Castle*, J. Livingston
__HP354 *Finding Courtney*, B. L. Etchison
__HP361 *The Name Game*, M. G. Chapman
__HP377 *Come Home to My Heart*, J. A. Grote
__HP378 *The Landlord Takes a Bride*, K. Billerbeck
__HP390 *Love Abounds*, A. Bell
__HP394 *Equestrian Charm*, D. Mills
__HP401 *Castle in the Clouds*, A. Boeshaar
__HP402 *Secret Ballot*, Y. Lehman
__HP405 *The Wife Degree*, A. Ford
__HP406 *Almost Twins*, G. Sattler
__HP409 *A Living Soul*, H. Alexander
__HP410 *The Color of Love*, D. Mills
__HP413 *Remnant of Victory*, J. Odell
__HP414 *The Sea Beckons*, B. L. Etchison
__HP417 *From Russia with Love*, C. Coble
__HP418 *Yesteryear*, G. Brandt
__HP421 *Looking for a Miracle*, W. E. Brunstetter
__HP422 *Condo Mania*, M. G. Chapman
__HP425 *Mustering Courage*, L. A. Coleman
__HP426 *To the Extreme*, T. Davis
__HP429 *Love Ahoy*, C. Coble
__HP430 *Good Things Come*, J. A. Ryan
__HP433 *A Few Flowers*, G. Sattler
__HP434 *Family Circle*, J. L. Barton
__HP438 *Out in the Real World*, K. Paul
__HP441 *Cassidy's Charm*, D. Mills
__HP442 *Vision of Hope*, M. H. Flinkman
__HP445 *McMillian's Matchmakers*, G. Sattler
__HP449 *An Ostrich a Day*, N. J. Farrier
__HP450 *Love in Pursuit*, D. Mills
__HP454 *Grace in Action*, K. Billerbeck
__HP458 *The Candy Cane Calaboose*, J. Spaeth

(If ordering from this page, please remember to include it with the order form.)

------- Presents -------

Great Inspirational Romance at a Great Price!

Heartsong Presents books are inspirational romances in contemporary and historical settings, designed to give you an enjoyable, spirit-lifting reading experience. You can choose wonderfully written titles from some of today's best authors like Hannah Alexander, Andrea Boeshaar, Yvonne Lehman, Tracie Peterson, and many others.

When ordering quantities less than twelve, above titles are $3.25 each.
Not all titles may be available at time of order.